Pinocchio

~

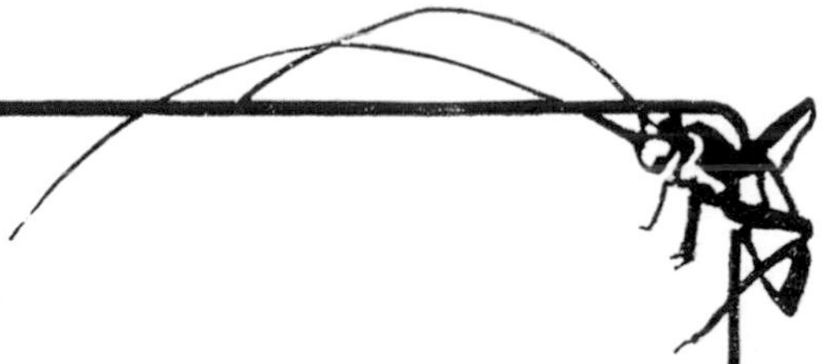

Pinocchio

~

A CLASSIC
ILLUSTRATED
EDITION

By Carlo Collodi

~

Compiled by
Cooper Edens

chronicle books·san francisco

For the Talking Cricket.—C.E.

This edition retains much of the content, spelling and
grammar of the original 1892 English language edition.

Compilation © 2001 by Blue Lantern Studio.
All rights reserved.

Book design by Kristen M. Nobles.
Typeset in Mrs. Eaves and Della Robbia.
Printed in Hong Kong.

Library of Congress Cataloging-in-Publication Data
Collodi, Carlo, 1826-1890.
        [Avventure di Pinocchio. English]
        Pinocchio / by Carlo Collodi ; compiled by Cooper Edens.
p. cm. -- (Classic illustrated treasury)
Summary: Presents the adventures of Pinocchio, a mischievous wooden
puppet, who wants more than anything else to become a real boy.
        ISBN 0-8118-2283-4
        [1. Fairy tales. 2. Puppets—Fiction.] I. Edens, Cooper. II. Title.
III. Series.
PZ8.C7 Ph 2001
[Fic]--dc21
    00-011497

Distributed in Canada by Raincoast Books
9050 Shaughnessy Street, Vancouver, British Columbia V6P 6E5

10 9 8 7 6 5 4 3 2 1

Chronicle Books LLC
85 Second Street, San Francisco, California 94105

www.chroniclebooks.com/Kids

~Preface~

amiliar with simplified versions of Carlo Collodi's classic nineteenth-century tale *Pinocchio*, I am surprised by the elegant and peculiar bizarreness of the complete and unedited story. I am especially amazed by the extraordinary vision and verve of the illustrators of the mischievous puppet who finally earns the distinction of being metamorphosed into a proper boy.

For this edition, I am fortunate to have been able to choose images from the works of such renowned illustrators as Italy's Enrico Mazzanti, Carlo Chiostri, Attilio Mussino and Luigi E. Maria Augusta Cavalieri; America's Maria L. Kirk, Alice Carsey and Frederick Richarson; and England's Charles Folkard. It has been a pleasure to experience the deep variety and rich expressionism of these brilliant artists, of whom many, like Chiostri, managed to bring "the fantastic" into the heart of reality, while others, like Cavalieri, moved in the opposite direction, and succeeded at making "the real" dreamlike.

I hope my collecting and arranging of the art binds the work of *Pinocchio's* many illustrators and Collodi's words into an original approach that pushes beyond the usual invention of this hyperkinetic marionette. I hope this edition offers the ambiguity and irony that make *Pinocchio* a thrilling ride through the most unusual landscapes and a strange adventure for all ages.

—Cooper Edens

~Table *of* Contents~

CHAPTER I

How it came to pass that Master Cherry the carpenter found a piece of wood that laughed and cried like a child.

There was once upon a time...

"A king!" my little readers will instantly exclaim.

No, children, you are wrong. There was once upon a time a piece of wood.

This wood was not valuable: it was only a common log like those that are burnt in winter in the stoves and fireplaces to make a cheerful blaze and warm the rooms.

I cannot say how it came about, but the fact is, that one fine day this piece of wood was lying in the shop of an old carpenter of the name of Master Anthony. He was, however, called by everybody Master Cherry, on account of the end of his nose, which was always as red and polished as a ripe cherry.

No sooner had Master Cherry set eyes on the piece of wood than his face beamed with delight; and, rubbing his hands together with satisfaction, he said softly to himself:

"This wood has come at the right moment; it will just do to make the leg of a little table."

Having said this he immediately took a sharp axe with which to remove the bark and the rough surface. Just, however, as he was going to give the first stroke he remained with his arm suspended in the air, for he heard a very small voice saying imploringly, "Do not strike me so hard!"

Picture to yourselves the astonishment of good old Master Cherry!

He turned his terrified eyes all round the room to try and discover where the little voice could possibly have come from, but he saw nobody! He looked under the bench—nobody; he looked into a cupboard that was always shut—nobody; he even opened the door of the shop and gave a glance into the street—and still nobody. Who, then, could it be?

"I see how it is," he said, laughing and scratching his wig; "evidently that little voice was all my imagination. Let us set to work again."

And taking up the axe he struck a tremendous blow on the piece of wood.

"Oh! oh! you have hurt me!" cried the same little voice dolefully.

This time Master Cherry was petrified. His eyes started out of his head with fright, his mouth remained open, and his tongue hung out almost to the end of his chin, like a mask on a fountain. As soon as he had recovered the use of his speech, he began to say, stuttering and trembling with fear:

"But where on earth can that little voice have come from that said 'Oh! oh!'?...Here there is certainly not a living soul. Is it possible that this piece of wood can have learnt to cry and to lament like a child? I cannot believe it. This piece of wood, here it is; a log for fuel like all the others, and thrown on the fire it would about suffice to boil a saucepan of beans.... How then? Can anyone be hidden inside it? If anyone is hidden inside, so much the worse for him. I will settle him at once."

So saying, he seized the poor piece of wood and commenced beating it without mercy against the walls of the room.

Then he stopped to listen if he could hear any little voice lamenting. He waited two minutes—nothing; five minutes—nothing; ten minutes—still nothing!

"I see how it is," he then said, forcing himself to laugh and pushing up his wig; "evidently the little voice that said 'Oh! oh!' was all my imagination! Let us set to work again."

But as all the same he was in a great fright, he tried to sing to give himself a little courage.

Putting the axe aside he took his plane, to plane and polish the bit of wood; but whilst he was running it up and down he heard the same little voice say, laughing:

"Have done! You are tickling me all over!"

This time poor Master Cherry fell down as if he had been struck by lightning. When he at last opened his eyes he found himself seated on the floor.

His face was quite changed, even the end of his nose, instead of being crimson, as it was nearly always, it had become blue from fright.

CHAPTER II

Geppetto takes the wood
to carve himself a marvelous puppet.

ust then there was a knock at the door.

"Come right in," said the carpenter, without strength enough to stand up.

Then into the workshop stepped a little old man, quite spry and perky, whose name was Geppetto; however, the boys of the neighborhood, when they wanted to drive him wild with rage, called him by the nickname Polendina on account of his yellow wig, which very much resembled polenta made with Indian corn.

Now, Geppetto was very hot-tempered. Woe if you called him Polendina! He'd fly off the handle, and there was no way of holding him down.

"Good day, Master Anthony," said Geppetto. "What are you doing there on the ground?"

"I'm teaching the ants how to count."

"Much good may it do you."

"Who brought you here, friend Geppetto?"

"My legs! Master Anthony, I must tell you that I've come to you for a favor."

"Here I am, at your service," replied the carpenter, climbing up on his knees.

"This morning an idea popped into my head."

"Let's hear it."

"I thought of making myself a fine wooden puppet; but a wonderful puppet who can dance, and fence, and make daredevil leaps. I intend to travel around the world with this puppet so as to earn my crust of bread and a glass of wine. What do you think about it?"

"Bravo, Polendina!" cried the same little voice that came from no one knew where.

On hearing himself called Polendina, friend Geppetto became as red with rage as a hot pepper, and turning on the carpenter, he said furiously:

"Why are you insulting me?"

"Who's insulting you?"

"You called me Polendina."

"It wasn't me."

"Then I suppose it was me! I say it was you."

"No!"

"Yes!"

And becoming more and more heated, they went from words to deeds, and grabbing one another they scratched, bit, and mauled each other.

When the battle was over, Master Anthony found himself with Geppetto's yellow wig in his hands, and Geppetto realized that he had the carpenter's grizzled wig in his mouth.

"Give me back my wig," shouted Master Anthony.

"And you give me back mine, then we'll make peace."

After each of them had got back his own wig, the two old men shook hands and swore to remain good friends for the rest of their lives.

"Now then, friend Geppetto," said the carpenter as a token of the peace they had made, "what's the favor you want from me?"

"I'd like some wood to make my puppet. Will you give it to me?" Delighted, Master Anthony went quickly to his workbench to get the piece of wood that had given him such an awful scare. But just as he was handing it over to his friend, the piece of wood gave a strong jolt, and, bolting suddenly out of his hands, banged against the thin and shriveled shins of poor Geppetto.

"Ah! So that's the courteous way you make a present of your goods? You've almost crippled me."

"I swear it wasn't me!"

"Then I suppose I did it."

"It's all the fault of this piece of wood."

"Liar!"

"Geppetto, don't insult me, or else I'll call you Polendina!..."

"Ass!"

"Polendina!"

"Jackass!"

"Polendina!"

"Baboon!"

"Polendina!"

Hearing himself called Polendina for the third time, Geppetto went wild and hurled himself at the carpenter; and right there they went at one another hammer and tongs.

When the battle was over, Master Anthony had two more scratches on his nose, and his foe had two buttons fewer on his jacket. Having evened the score in this way, they shook hands and swore to remain good friends for the rest of their lives.

And so Geppetto took his precious piece of wood with him, and having thanked Master Anthony, he hobbled on home.

After returning home, Geppetto begins at once to make his puppet and names him Pinocchio. The puppet plays his first pranks.

eppetto's home was a small room on the ground floor that got its light from the areaway under a staircase. The furnishings couldn't have been more modest: a rickety chair, a broken-down bed and a battered table. At the back wall you could see a fireplace with a fire burning; but it was a painted fire, and along with the fire there was painted a kettle that boiled merrily and sent up a cloud of steam that really looked like steam.

Once inside, Geppetto immediately got his tools and began to carve and shape his puppet.

"What name shall I give him?" he said to himself. "I'll call him Pinocchio. The name will bring him good luck. I once knew a whole family of Pinocchios: the father was a Pinocchio, the mother was a Pinocchia, and the children were Pinocchios. And they all did well for themselves. The richest one of them begged for a living."

Having found a name for his puppet, he then began to work in earnest, and quickly made his hair, then his forehead, and then his eyes.

When the eyes were done, just imagine his astonishment when he realized that those eyes moved and that they were staring him straight in the face.

Seeing himself looked at by those two eyes of wood, Geppetto took a little offense and said in an irritated tone:

"Spiteful wooden eyes, why are you looking at me?"

Nobody answered.

Then, after the eyes he made him a nose. But as soon as the nose was made, it began to grow; and it grew and grew and grew so that in a few minutes it became an endless nose.

Poor Geppetto kept struggling to cut it back; but the more he cut and shortened it, the longer that impudent nose became.

After the nose he made him a mouth.

The mouth wasn't even done when it quickly began to laugh and mock him. "Stop laughing!" said Geppetto out of sorts; but it was like talking to the wall. "Stop laughing, I repeat!" he roared in a threatening voice.

The mouth stopped laughing then; but it stuck its tongue out all the way.

So as not to spoil what he was doing, Geppetto pretended not to notice this and went on working. After the mouth, he made his chin, then his neck, then his shoulders, his trunk, his arms and his hands.

As soon as the hands were finished, Geppetto felt his wig being snatched from his head. He looked up, and what did he see? He saw his yellow wig in the puppet's hands.

"Pinocchio!…give me back my wig at once."

But instead of giving back the wig, Pinocchio put it on his own head, nearly suffocating underneath it.

At that insolent and mocking behavior, Geppetto became sadder and more dejected than he had ever been in his life; and turning to Pinocchio, he said:

"Scamp of a child, you aren't even finished and you're already beginning to lack respect for your father! That's bad, my boy, bad!"

And he wiped away a tear.

The legs and feet still remained to be done.

When Geppetto finished making him feet, he felt a kick land on the tip of his nose.

"I deserve it!" he said to himself then. "I should have thought of it before; now it's too late."

Then he took the puppet under his arms and put him down on the floor of the room in order to make him walk.

Pinocchio's legs were stiff, and he didn't know how to move; so Geppetto led him by the hand, teaching him how to take one step after the other.

When his legs were limbered, Pinocchio began to walk on his own and then to run around the room; and then, having rushed out the door, he jumped into the street and set off on the run.

And there was poor Geppetto running after him without being able to catch up, because that imp of a Pinocchio bounded along like a hare; and as his wooden feet struck the pavement, he made a clatter like twenty pairs of peasants' clogs.

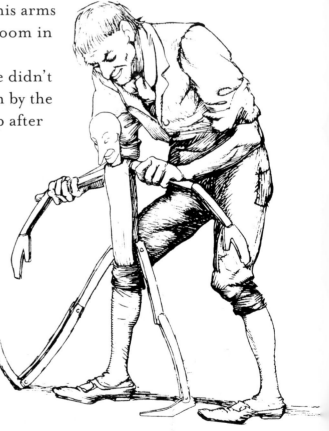

"Catch him! Catch him!" shouted Geppetto; but the passersby, seeing a wooden puppet running like a racehorse, just stood still in amazement to watch him, and laughed and laughed and laughed beyond belief.

At last, by a lucky chance, a carabiniere happened along. Hearing all that racket and thinking it was a colt running wildly out of control, he set himself bravely with legs wide apart in the middle of the street, determined to stop it and prevent anything worse from happening.

But when Pinocchio, from a distance, noticed that the carabiniere was blocking the whole street, he planned to surprise him by passing between his legs; but he botched it.

Without budging at all, the carabiniere snatched him neatly by the nose (it was an enormously long nose that seemed made expressly to be seized by carabinieri) and handed him over to Geppetto who, for the sake of discipline, immediately wanted to box his ears. But just imagine how he felt when, looking for his ears, he wasn't able to find them. And do you know why? Because in his haste to carve him, he had forgotten to make them.

So he took him by the scruff of the neck, and as he led him back he said, shaking his head threateningly:

"Let's go straight home. And when we're home, you can be sure that we'll settle our accounts!"

Hearing this tune, Pinocchio threw himself to the ground and refused to walk any further. Meanwhile the curious and the idlers began to stop and gather around them in a group.

Some said one thing; some said another.

"Poor puppet," some said, "he's right not to want to go home. Who knows how that awful Geppetto would beat him!"

And the others added maliciously:

"That Geppetto looks like a good man, but he's a real tyrant with children. If they leave that poor puppet in his hands, he's more than capable of hacking him to pieces."

In short, they made such a hue and cry that the carabiniere set Pinocchio free again and marched poor old Geppetto off to prison. And he, not finding words to defend himself just then, cried like a calf; and on the way to jail he stammered amid his sobbing:

"Wicked child! And to think that I worked so hard to make him into a nice puppet! But it serves me right. I should have known better."

What happened afterward is so strange a story that it is hardly to be believed; but I will tell you about it in the following chapters.

CHAPTER IV

The story of Pinocchio and the Talking Cricket, wherein we see that bad boys don't like to be corrected by those who know better than they do.

So, children, I will tell you that while poor Geppetto was being led blameless to prison, that little urchin Pinocchio was no sooner out of the claws of the carabiniere than he took to his heels, cutting across the fields in order to get back home more quickly. And in his great haste, he jumped over high embankments, briar hedges, and gushing streams, just like a kid-goat or a young hare chased by hunters.

When he arrived in front of the house he found the street door ajar, so he pushed it open and went in; and as soon as he had bolted the door tight, he sat plunk on the floor, heaving a deep sigh of satisfaction.

But his satisfaction didn't last long, for he heard someone in the room go: "Crick-crick-crick."

"Who's calling me?" said Pinocchio, thoroughly frightened.

"It is I."

Pinocchio turned around and saw a large Cricket crawling slowly up the wall.

"Tell me, Cricket, just who are you?"

"I'm the Talking Cricket, and I've lived in this room for over a hundred years."

"Now, however, this room is mine," said the puppet, "and if you want to do me a real favor, get out of here right away without even looking back."

"I will not go from here," replied the Cricket, "without first telling you a great truth."

"Tell me and hurry up."

"Woe to those children who disobey their parents and willfully leave home. They will never come to any good in this world, and sooner or later they'll be bitterly sorry for it."

"Sing on all you want, my dear Cricket; but I know that I'm going away tomorrow at dawn, because if I stay here, what happens to all the other kids will happen to me. I mean to say that they'll send me to school, and whether I like it or not I'll have to study; but confidentially, I don't have the slightest desire to study, and I get more pleasure from chasing butterflies and climbing up trees to get baby birds."

"Poor little simpleton! Don't you know that if you do that, you'll grow up to be a perfect jackass and everyone will poke fun at you?"

"Shut up, wretched Cricket of doom!" shouted Pinocchio.

But the Cricket, who was both patient and a philosopher, instead of taking offense at such impudence, went on in the same tone of voice:

"And if it doesn't suit you to go to school, why don't you at least learn a trade so that you can earn your slice of bread honestly?"

"Do you want me to tell you why?" replied Pinocchio, who was beginning to lose his temper. "Of all the trades in the world there's really only one that's to my liking."

"And what trade would that be?"

"That of eating, drinking, sleeping, having fun, and living the life of a vagabond from morning to night."

"For your information," said the Talking Cricket with his usual calm, "everyone who follows that trade is bound to end up in the poorhouse or in prison."

"Watch out, wretched Cricket of doom! If I get mad, it'll be too bad for you."

"Poor Pinocchio, I really feel sorry for you."

"Why do you feel sorry for me?"

"Because you're a puppet and, what's worse, because you've got a wooden head."

At these words, Pinocchio jumped up in a fury, and taking a mallet from the workbench, he hurled it at the Talking Cricket.

Maybe he didn't even mean to hit him, but unluckily he caught him squarely on the head, so that the poor Cricket barely had enough breath to utter a crick-crick-crick, after which he remained there stark dead and stuck on the wall.

CHAPTER V

Pinocchio gets hungry and looks for an egg to make himself an omelette; but lo and behold, the omelette flies away from him and out the window.

In the meantime night started to fall, and remembering that he hadn't eaten anything, Pinocchio felt a little pang in his stomach that very much resembled a twinge of appetite.

But a child's appetite grows fast, and in fact after a few minutes his appetite became hunger; and in the twinkle of an eye he had become as hungry as a wolf: a hunger so thick that you could cut it with a knife.

Poor Pinocchio ran quickly to the hearth where a kettle was boiling and reached out to uncover it so as to see what was in it; but the kettle was painted on the wall. You can imagine how he felt. His nose, which was already long, grew still longer by at least some four inches.

Then he began to run around the room, rummaging in all the drawers and nooks and corners, looking for a piece of bread, even stale bread, a small crust, a bone left by a dog, a bit of moldy polenta, a fish bone, a cherry pit: in short, something to chew on. But he found nothing, a whole lot of nothing, plain nothing.

And meanwhile his hunger grew and grew all the time; but the only relief poor Pinocchio got came from yawning. He yawned so wide that sometimes his mouth opened as far back as his ears; and after yawning, he would spit, until he felt as if his stomach were caving in.

Then, weeping in despair, he said:

"The Talking Cricket was right. I was wrong to rebel against my father and run away from home.... If my father were here now, I wouldn't be yawning to death. Oh, what an awful sickness hunger is!"

But just then he thought he saw on top of the rubbish pile something round and white that looked quite like a hen's egg. In a flash he leaped and pounced on it. It really was an egg.

It's impossible to describe the puppet's joy; you have to be able to imagine it. Almost thinking it was a dream, he turned the egg over and over in his hands, fondling it and kissing it; and as he kissed it, he said:

"And now how shall I cook it? I'll make an omelette with it...no, it's better to cook it on a griddle...but wouldn't it be tastier if I fried it in a skillet? What if, instead, I made a soft-boiled egg? No, the fastest way of all is to cook it on a griddle or in a small pan. I can't wait to eat it."

No sooner said than done. He put a small pan on a brazier full of burning embers; in place of butter and oil he put a little water in the pan, and when the water began to steam, crack! He broke the shell of the egg and started to drop it in.

But instead of the white of the egg and the yolk, a little chick all perky and ceremonious jumped out and, making a fine bow, said:

"A thousand thanks, Signor Pinocchio, for saving me the trouble of breaking the shell. Bye, bye, for now; keep well, and best regards to all at home."

Having said this, he spread his wings and, passing through the open window, flew away far out of sight.

The poor puppet stood there as if bewitched, eyes gaping, mouth wide open, and the two halves of the eggshell in his hands. However, when he had recovered from the first shock, he began to cry, to scream, to stamp his feet on the ground in desperation; and weeping all the time, he said:

"The Talking Cricket was really right, then. If I hadn't run away and if my father were here now, I wouldn't be starving to death. Oh! What an awful sickness hunger is!"

And because his stomach went on grumbling more than ever and he didn't know what to do to quiet it, he decided to make a quick dash to the nearby village in the hope of finding some kind person who might give him a bit of bread.

CHAPTER VI

Pinocchio falls asleep with his feet on the brazier and wakes up the next morning with his feet all burned off.

t so happened that it was a horrid, hellish night. It thundered mightily, lightning flashed as though the sky were catching fire, and a cold, blustery wind whistled wildly as it raised a huge cloud of dust and made all the trees in the countryside screech and creak.

Pinocchio was terribly afraid of thunder and lightning. But his hunger was stronger than his fear. So he set the door ajar, and going at full speed, in about a hundred leaps and bounds he reached the village, panting heavily and with his tongue hanging out, just like a hunting dog.

But he found everything dark and deserted. The shops were closed; the doors were closed; the windows were closed; and not even a stray dog was in the streets. It looked like the land of the dead.

Driven by despair and hunger, Pinocchio then tugged at the bellcord of a house and rang uninterruptedly, telling himself:

"Someone is bound to look out."

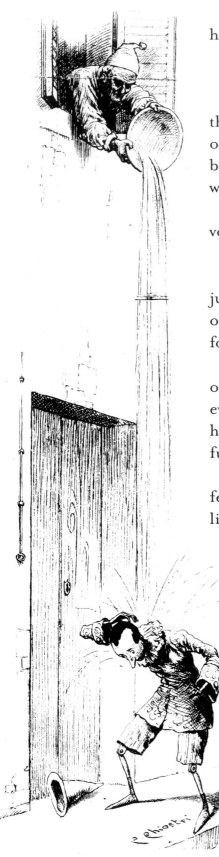

In fact, a little old man with a nightcap on his head looked out the window and shouted angrily:

"What do you want at this hour?"

"Would you be so kind as to give me some bread?"

"Wait where you are; I'll be right back," answered the little old man, thinking that he had to do with one of those young rowdies who amuse themselves at night by ringing doorbells just to annoy respectable people who are sleeping peacefully.

In half a minute the window opened again, and the voice of that same little old man called out to Pinocchio:

"Come closer and hold out your hat."

Pinocchio took off his shabby little hat at once, but just as he was holding it out, he felt an enormous basinful of water pour down on him, drenching him from head to foot as though he were a pot of withering geraniums.

He returned home wet as a chick and quite worn out with fatigue and hunger; and because he no longer even had the strength to stand up, he sat down, putting his soaked and mud-spattered feet on top of a brazier full of burning embers.

And there he fell asleep; and while he slept his feet, which were made of wood, caught fire and little by little burned and turned to ashes.

But Pinocchio went on sleeping and snoring as though his feet belonged to someone else. Finally, at daybreak he woke up because somebody had knocked at the door.

"Who is it?" he asked, yawning and rubbing his eyes.

"It's me!" answered a voice.

It was the voice of Geppetto.

CHAPTER VII

Geppetto returns home and gives the puppet the breakfast that the poor man had brought for himself.

oor Pinocchio, whose eyes were still sleepy, hadn't yet realized that his feet were all burned off; so as soon as he heard his father's voice he jumped down from his stool in order to run and unbolt the door; but after two or three lurches all at once he fell flat on the floor.

And in striking the floor, he made the same racket that a sackful of wooden ladles would have made in falling from the fifth story.

"Open up for me!" Geppetto shouted meanwhile from the street.

"Dear father, I can't," replied the puppet, crying and rolling about on the floor.

"Why can't you?"

"Because they've eaten my feet."

"Who ate them?"

"The cat," said Pinocchio, seeing the cat who was amusing itself by kicking up some wood shavings with its front paws.

"Let me in, I say!" repeated Geppetto. "If not, when I get in I'll give you the cat all right!"

"I can't stand up, believe me. Oh, poor me, poor me. I'll have to walk on my knees all my life!"

Thinking that all that whining was another of the puppet's pranks, Geppetto decided to put a stop to it; so, climbing up the wall, he entered the house by the window.

At first he had intended to treat him harshly, but when he saw his very own Pinocchio stretched out on the floor and really without feet, he felt his heart melt, and quickly picking him up in his arms, he kissed and fondled him with a thousand blandishments. And as big tears rolled down his cheeks, he said amidst his sobbing:

"My poor little Pinocchio, how is it that you burned your feet off?"

"I don't know, father, but believe me, it was a hellish night, and I'll remember it as long as I live. It was thundering and lightning and I was very hungry, and then the Talking Cricket said to me, 'It serves you right; you've been wicked, and you deserve it,' and I said to him, 'Watch out, Cricket!' and he said to me, 'You're a puppet and you've got a wooden head,' and I threw a mallet at him and he died, but it was his fault, because I didn't want to kill him, the proof being that I put a little pan on the burning embers of the brazier, but the chick jumped out and said: 'Bye-bye and best regards to all at home,' and I got more and more hungry, on account of which that little old man with the nightcap, looking out the window, said to me: 'Come closer and hold out your hat,' and with that basinful of water on my head (it's not a disgrace to ask for a piece of bread, is it?) I returned home, and because I was still very hungry I put my feet on the brazier to dry out, and you came back and I found them burned off, and in the meantime I'm still hungry and my feet are all gone. Boo...hoo...hoo!..."

And poor Pinocchio began to cry and wail so loudly that they could hear him five miles away.

Geppetto understood only one thing in all that rigamarole, and that is that the puppet was dying of hunger; so he took three pears from his pocket, and handing them over to him he said:

"These three pears were for my breakfast, but I'm glad to give them to you. Eat them, and may they do you good."

"If you want me to eat them, do me the favor of peeling them."

"Peeling them?" replied Geppetto, taken aback. "My boy, I would never have believed that you were so fussy and finicky. That's bad! In this world, from the time we are children we have to get used to eating any-thing and everything, because we never know what may befall us. So many things can happen!"

"You may be right," Pinocchio retorted, "but I'll never eat fruit that's not peeled. I can't stand the skins."

And so good old Geppetto took out a small knife, and fortifying himself with saintly patience he peeled the three pears, putting the skins on the corner of the table.

After he had eaten the first pear in just two bites, Pinocchio was about to throw away the core; but Geppetto held back his arm and said:

"Don't throw it away: in this world everything may come in handy."

"But I am certainly not going to eat the core," the puppet yelled, recoiling like a viper.

"Who knows! So many things can happen...." Geppetto said again, without losing his temper.

And so the three cores, instead of being thrown out the window, were placed on the corner of the table along with the peelings.

Having eaten, or rather devoured, the three pears, Pinocchio gave a long and deep yawn and whimpered:

"I'm still hungry."

"But, my child, I don't have anything else to give you."

"Really, nothing at all?"

"All I have are these pear cores and peelings."

"Patience!" said Pinocchio. "If there's nothing else, I'll eat some peelings."

And he began to chew on them. At first he made faces; but then one after another he polished off all the peelings, and after the peelings the cores too. And when he had finished eating everything, he clapped his stomach with satisfaction and said gleefully:

"Now I feel better."

"So you see," Geppetto remarked, "I was right when I told you that we shouldn't become too choosy or too finicky in our tastes. My dear boy, we can never be sure about what may befall us in this world. So many things can happen!"

CHAPTER VIII

Geppetto makes new feet for Pinocchio and sells his own jacket to buy him a spelling book.

As soon as he satisfied his hunger, the puppet began to grumble and cry, because he wanted a new pair of feet.

But Geppetto, to punish him for the mischief he had done, let him cry and wail for half a day. Then he said to him:

"And why should I make your feet over again? So I can see you run away from home again?"

"I promise," said the puppet, sobbing, "that from now on I'll be good."

"All children, when they want something, say the same thing," replied Geppetto.

"I promise that I'll go to school, I'll study and make you proud of me."

"All children, when they want something, repeat the same story."

"But I'm not like other children! I'm better than all of them, and I always tell the truth. I promise you, father, that I'll learn a trade and be the comfort and staff of your old age."

Although he put on a tyrant's look, Geppetto's eyes filled with tears and his heart swelled with compassion on seeing his poor Pinocchio in such a pitiful state. So he said nothing more; but taking up his tools and two small pieces of seasoned wood, he set to work in the greatest earnest.

And in less than an hour the feet were all done; two nimble little feet, slender and sinewy, as though carved by a supreme artist.

Then Geppetto said to the puppet:

"Close your eyes and go to sleep."

So he closed his eyes and pretended to sleep. And while Pinocchio pretended to be sleeping, Geppetto took some glue he had melted in an eggshell and stuck the feet in place; and he stuck them on so well that you couldn't even see any sign of the seam.

As soon as the puppet realized that he had feet, he jumped down from the table where he had been lying and started to skip and caper all around as though he had gone wild with joy.

"To pay you back for all you've done for me," Pinocchio said to his father, "I'll start school right away."

"Splendid, my boy!"

"But to go to school I need some clothes."

Geppetto, who was poor and didn't even have a penny in his pocket, then made him a modest little suit out of flowered paper, a pair of shoes out of tree bark, and a cap out of bread crumb.

Pinocchio immediately ran to look at himself in a basin full of water and felt so pleased with himself that he said, as proud as a peacock:

"I look like a real gentleman!"

"Quite so," replied Geppetto. "Because, and keep this in mind, it's not fine clothes that make a gentleman, but clean ones."

"By the way," the puppet continued, "to go to school, there's still something I need; in fact, I lack the most important and most necessary thing of all."

"And what's that?"

"I don't have a spelling book."

"You're right; but how can we get one?"

"It's quite easy; we'll go to a bookstore and buy one."

"And the money?"

"I don't have any."

"Neither have I," added the good old man, saddened.

And although Pinocchio was a very good-humored boy, even he became sad, because poverty, when it is true poverty, is understood by everyone, even by children.

"Never mind!" Geppetto exclaimed all of a sudden, getting to his feet; and slipping on his old fustian jacket full of darns and patches, he rushed out of the house.

After a short while he returned; and when he returned, he was holding the spelling book for his son in his hands, but he no longer had his jacket. The poor man was in shirt sleeves, and it was snowing outside.

"And your jacket, father?"

"I sold it."

"Why did you sell it?"

"Because it made me hot."

Pinocchio caught the meaning of this answer at once, and being unable to restrain his heart's true impulse, he threw his arms around Geppetto's neck and covered his face with kisses.

CHAPTER IX

Pinocchio sells his spelling book in order to go and see the puppet show.

hen it had stopped snowing, Pinocchio, with his fine new spelling book under his arm, set out for school, and on the way his little head dreamed up a thousand thoughts and built a thousand castles in the air, each more beautiful than the last.

And talking to himself, he said:

"Today, at school, I'll learn how to read right away, tomorrow I'll learn how to write, and the day after tomorrow I'll learn arithmetic. Then with my skill I'll make lots of money, and with the first money that I get in my pocket I'll buy my father a beautiful woolen jacket. But what am I talking about, wool? I'll get him one all of silver and gold, with diamond buttons. And the poor man really deserves it, because, after all, in order to buy me books and have me educated he's left in shirt sleeves...in the middle of winter! Only fathers are capable of such sacrifices."

While, greatly moved, he was saying this, he thought he heard in the distance a music of fifes and the thump of a bass drum: fi-fi-fi, fi-fi-fi, boom, boom, boom.

He stopped and stood listening. The sounds came from the other end of a very long crossroad that led to a small village built by the seashore.

"What can that music be? It's too bad I have to go to school; otherwise...."

And he stood there, undecided. Nonetheless, it was necessary for him to make a decision: to go to school or to listen to the fifes.

"Today I'll go and hear the fifes, and tomorrow I'll go to school. There's always time to go to school," the little scamp finally said, shrugging his shoulders.

Without further ado, he took the crossroad and began to run hard. The more he ran, the more distinctly he heard the sound of the fifes and the thump of the bass drum: fi-fi-fi, fi-fi-fi, fi-fi-fi, boom, boom, boom, boom.

And suddenly he found himself in the middle of a square full of people crowding around a large booth made of wood and canvas painted in a thousand colors.

"What's that large booth?" asked Pinocchio, turning to a small boy who was from the village.

"Read the poster where it's written, and you'll know."

"I'd like to read it, but it just so happens that today I can't read."

"Good for you, dumb ox! Then I'll read it to you. For your information, on that poster with flaming-red letters it says: GREAT PUPPET SHOW."

"Is it long since the show began?"

"It's just beginning now."

"How much does it cost to get in?"

"Four pennies."

Pinocchio, who was burning with curiosity, lost all reserve, and without feeling ashamed he asked the small boy with whom he was talking:

"Would you give me four pennies until tomorrow?"

"I'd be glad to give them to you," the other boy answered, mocking him, "but it just so happens that today I can't give them to you."

"I'll sell you my jacket for four pennies," the puppet said to him then.

"What do you expect me to do with a jacket of flowered paper? If it rains on it, there's no way of taking it off."

"Do you want to buy my shoes?"

"They're only good for lighting a fire."

"How much will you give me for my cap?"

"A great bargain, for sure! A cap made of bread crumb! The chances are that the mice would come and eat it right off my head."

Pinocchio was on pins and needles. He was on the verge of making a final offer, but he didn't have the heart; he hesitated, wavered, writhed with anguish. At last he said:

"Will you give me four pennies for this new spelling book?"

"I'm just a boy, and I don't buy anything from other boys," replied his little interlocutor who had more sense than he had.

"For four pennies I'll take the spelling book," cried out a ragman who had been present during the conversation.

And so the book was sold right there on the spot. And to think that poor old Geppetto had remained at home shivering with cold in his shirt sleeves just to buy that spelling book for his son!

CHAPTER X

The puppets recognize their brother Pinocchio and give him a joyous welcome; but just then the puppeteer, Fire-Eater, turns up and Pinocchio runs the risk of coming to a bad end.

When Pinocchio entered the puppet theater, an incident occurred that caused a near riot.

First, you have to know that the curtain was already up and the show had already begun.

On the stage Harlequin and Punchinello were seen quarreling with one another, and as usual were threatening to exchange a load of slaps and thwacks at any moment.

The spectators, completely absorbed, laughed so hard that it hurt as they listened to the squabble of the two puppets who were gesticulating and insulting each other as realistically as if they were two rational beings of this world.

But all of a sudden, just like that, Harlequin stopped acting and, turning toward the audience and pointing to someone in the rear of the pit, began to exclaim melodramatically:

"Gods above! Do I wake or dream? But surely that is Pinocchio down there."

"It's really Pinocchio," yelled Punchinello.

"It's actually him," screamed Signora Rosaura, peeping out from the back of the stage.

"It's Pinocchio! It's Pinocchio!" shouted all the puppets in chorus, leaping out from the wings. "It's Pinocchio! It's our brother Pinocchio! Long live Pinocchio!"

"Pinocchio, come up here to me!" shouted Harlequin, "come and throw yourself into the arms of your brothers-in-wood!"

At this warm invitation Pinocchio made a bound from the back of the pit to the front section; then with another bound, from the front section he landed on the head of the orchestra conductor; and from there he sprang onto the stage.

It's impossible to imagine all the hugging, the tight clasps around the neck, the friendly pinches and the raps on the head given in true brotherly affection, that Pinocchio received in the midst of all that confusion from the actors and actresses of the puppet theater company.

It was a moving sight, no doubt about it; but the audience, seeing that the show wasn't getting on, became restless and began to yell:

"On with the show! On with the show!"

It was all a waste of breath, because instead of going on with the performance, the puppets redoubled the fracas and their shouts; and raising Pinocchio up on their shoulders, they carried him in triumph before the footlights.

But then the puppeteer came out, a man so huge and ugly that just to look at him gave one a fright. He had a fearsome beard, as black as an inkblot and so long that it reached from his chin down to the ground. Just think, he stepped on it when he walked! His mouth was as wide as an oven, his eyes looked like two lanterns of red glass with the flame burning inside them, and in his hands he held a big whip (which he would crack) made of snakes and foxtails twisted together.

At the unexpected appearance of the puppeteer, everyone turned mute; no one even breathed anymore. You could have heard a fly go by. Those poor puppets, male and female alike, trembled like so many leaves in the wind.

"What do you mean by coming here to create a riot in my theater?" the puppeteer asked Pinocchio, in the booming voice of an ogre with a bad head cold.

"Believe me, most illustrious Sir, it wasn't my fault."

"That's enough! We'll settle our accounts tonight."

In fact, when the performance was over, the puppeteer went into the kitchen where a fine large sheep he had prepared himself for dinner was slowly turning on the spit. Now, because he lacked the firewood to finish roasting and browning it, he called Harlequin and Punchinello and said to them:

"Bring me the puppet that you'll find hanging on the nail. It seems to me that he's a puppet made of very dry wood, and if I throw him on the fire I'm sure he'll make a beautiful blaze for the roast."

At first Harlequin and Punchinello hesitated, but being terrified at the fierce look of their master, they obeyed; and in a little while they came back into the kitchen carrying poor Pinocchio, who was wriggling like an eel out of water and screaming desperately:

"Dear Father, save me! I don't want to die, no, I don't want to die."

CHAPTER XI

Fire-Eater sneezes and forgives Pinocchio, who then saves his friend Harlequin from death.

he puppeteer Fire-Eater (for that was his name) seemed a fearsome man, I don't deny it, especially with that awful black beard of his, which covered all his chest and legs like an apron; but deep down he wasn't a bad man. The proof is that as soon as he saw poor Pinocchio brought before him, struggling as hard as he could and screaming: "I don't want to die, I don't want to die!" he was immediately touched and began to feel pity for him. And after having resisted for quite awhile, he just couldn't stand it any longer and let out a powerful sneeze.

At that sneeze Harlequin, who until then had been dejected and drooping like a weeping willow tree, showed a cheerful face, and leaning toward Pinocchio he whispered softly:

"Good news, brother! The puppeteer sneezed, and that's a sign that he's taking pity on you. So now you're saved."

Because, you see, whereas all other persons who feel sorry for someone either cry or at least pretend to dry their tears, whenever Fire-Eater was really touched, he had the bad habit of sneezing. It was as good a way as another of letting people know he had a heart with feelings.

After he had sneezed, the puppeteer, continuing to appear grumpy, shouted at Pinocchio:

"Stop crying! Your wailing has given me a funny feeling in the pit of my stomach.... I feel a spasm, that almost, almost...atchoo! atchoo!" and he sneezed again twice.

"Bless you!" said Pinocchio.

"Thank you! And your father and mother, are they still alive?" Fire-Eater asked him.

"My father is; but I never knew my mother."

"Who knows how grieved your old father would be if I had thrown you on those burning coals! Poor old man, I feel sorry for him!...Atchoo, atchoo, atchoo!" and he sneezed three more times.

"Bless you!" said Pinocchio.

"Thank you! All the same, you have to feel sorry for me too, because as you can see I don't have any more firewood to finish roasting my mutton, and to tell the truth, in these circumstances you would have been a great convenience to me. But now I've been moved to pity and that's that. Instead of you, I'll have a puppet from my company burned on the spit. Ho there, gendarmes!"

At this command, two wooden gendarmes appeared on the spot, very tall and lean, with three-cornered hats on their heads and unsheathed swords in their hands.

Then the puppeteer said to them in a wheezing voice:

"Seize Harlequin there, tie him up tight, and then throw him on the fire to burn. I want my mutton to be well roasted."

Imagine poor Harlequin! He was so terrified that his legs folded under him and he fell flat on his face.

At that heartrending sight, Pinocchio threw himself at the puppeteer's feet, weeping in torrents and drenching the hair of that enormously long beard. Then he said in a pleading voice:

"Have pity, Signor Fire-Eater!"

"There are no signori here," replied the puppeteer harshly.

"Have pity, Sir Knight!"

"There are no knights here."

"Have pity, Sir Commendatore!"

"There are no commendatori here."

"Have pity, Excellency!"

On hearing himself called Excellency, the puppeteer quickly pursed his lips, and suddenly becoming more gentle and affable, he said to Pinocchio:

"Well then, what do you want of me?"

"I beg mercy of you for poor Harlequin."

"There's no place for mercy here. Since I've spared you, I must have him put on the fire, because I want my mutton to be well roasted."

"In that case," cried Pinocchio boldly, getting up and throwing off his cap of crumb, "in that case I know where my duty lies. Come gendarmes! Bind me and throw me on those flames there. No, it is not right that poor Harlequin, my true friend, should die for me."

These words, uttered in a clear, heroic tone, made all the puppets present at that scene cry. Even the gendarmes, although they were made of wood, cried like two newborn lambs.

At first, Fire-Eater remained hard and unyielding, like a block of ice; but then he too began slowly to melt and then to sneeze. And after four or five sneezes, he opened his arms affectionately and said to Pinocchio:

"You're really a wonderful lad. Come here and give me a kiss."

Pinocchio ran quickly, and scampering up the puppeteer's beard like a squirrel, he planted a hearty kiss on the tip of his nose.

"Mercy is granted then?" asked poor Harlequin, in a faint voice that could hardly be heard.

"Mercy is granted," answered Fire-Eater; then, with a sigh as he shook his head, he added:

"So be it! For tonight I'll resign myself to eating my mutton half-cooked; but the next time it'll be too bad for whoever happens to come along."

At the news that mercy had been obtained, all the puppets ran onto the stage, and having lit the lamps and chandeliers as if for an evening gala performance, they began to leap and dance. Dawn came, and they were still dancing.

CHAPTER XII

The puppeteer, Fire-Eater, gives Pinocchio five gold pieces to take to his father Geppetto; but Pinocchio lets himself be duped by the Fox and the Cat and goes off with them.

The next day Fire-Eater called Pinocchio to one side and asked him:

"What's your father's name?"

"Geppetto."

"And what's his trade?"

"That of a poor man."

"Does he earn much?"

"He earns enough never to have a cent in his pocket. Just think that in order to buy me a spelling book for school he had to sell the only jacket he had; a jacket so full of darns and patches that it was a calamity."

"Poor devil, I almost feel sorry for him. Here's five gold coins. Go and take them to him right away, and give him my best wishes."

As you can well imagine, Pinocchio thanked the puppeteer a thousand times. He embraced all the puppets of the company one by one, even the gendarmes, and then, beside himself with joy, he set out for home.

But he hadn't yet gone half a mile when he met a Fox, lame in one foot, and a Cat, blind in both eyes, who were making their way very slowly, helping one another like good comrades in misfortune. The Fox, who was lame, walked leaning on the Cat, and the Cat, who was blind, was led by the Fox.

"Good day, Pinocchio," said the Fox, greeting him politely.
"How is it that you know my name?" asked the puppet.
"I know your father well."
"Where did you last see him?"
"I saw him yesterday in the doorway of his house."

"And what was he doing?"

"He was in shirt sleeves, shivering with cold."

"Poor father! But, God willing, from now on he won't shiver any more."

"Why not?"

"Because I've become a wealthy man."

"A wealthy man, you?" said the Fox, and he began to laugh in a coarse and mocking manner. And the Cat was laughing too, but so as not to show it he stroked his whiskers with his forepaws.

"There's nothing to laugh at," cried Pinocchio, peevishly. "I'm really sorry to make your mouths water, but these, if you know anything about it, are five beautiful gold coins."

And he pulled out the coins he had received as a gift from Fire-Eater.

At the agreeable ring of those coins, the Fox, with an involuntary movement, stretched out the paw that was supposed to be crippled, and the Cat opened both eyes so wide that they looked like two green lanterns; but then he closed them again so quickly that Pinocchio didn't notice anything.

"And now," the Fox asked him, "what do you expect to do with those coins of yours?"

"First of all," the puppet answered, "I intend to buy my father a fine new jacket made all of gold and silver, and with diamond buttons; and then I want to buy a spelling book for myself."

"For yourself?"

"That's right. Because I want to go to school and study hard."

"Look at me!" said the Fox. "Because of a foolish passion for study I lost a paw."

"Look at me!" said the Cat. "Because of a foolish passion for study I lost the sight of both eyes."

At that moment a White Blackbird, who was perched on the hedge by the road, began his usual chirping and said:

"Pinocchio, don't listen to the advice of bad companions, or you'll regret it!"

Poor Blackbird, would that he had never said it! With a sudden leap the Cat pounced on him and without even giving him the time to say "oh" devoured him in one gulp, feathers and all.

After he had eaten him and wiped his mouth, the Cat closed his eyes again and began once more to pretend that he was blind as before.

"Poor Blackbird," said Pinocchio to the Cat, "why did you treat him so badly?"

"I did it to teach him a lesson. Now the next time he'll know better than to stick his beak into other people's affairs."

They had gone more than halfway to Geppetto's house, when all of a sudden the Fox stopped and said to the puppet:

"Do you want to double your gold coins?"

"What do you mean?"

"Do you want to turn those miserable five gold pieces into a hundred or a thousand or two thousand?"

"You bet! But how?"

"The way to do it is quite easy. Instead of going back home, you'd only have to come with us."

"And where do you want to take me?"

"To Dodoland."

Pinocchio thought about it for a moment, and then said resolutely:

"No, I won't come. I'm nearly home now, and I want to continue home where my father's waiting for me. Who knows how sad the poor old man was yesterday not seeing me come back. Unfortunately, I've been a bad son, and the Talking Cricket was right when he said: 'Disobedient children can't come to any good in this world.' And I've learned it the hard way, because a lot of bad things have happened to me; and just last night in Fire-Eater's house I was in danger of...brrr! I get goose pimples just thinking of it!"

"So then," the Fox said, "you really want to go home? Well, go ahead then, and so much the worse for you."

"So much the worse for you!" repeated the Cat.

"Think it over, Pinocchio, because you're throwing away a golden opportunity."

"A golden opportunity!" repeated the Cat.

"Your five gold pieces could have become two thousand overnight."

"Two thousand!" repeated the Cat.

"But how is it possible for them to become that many?" asked Pinocchio, his mouth agape in astonishment.

"I'll explain it to you right away," said the Fox. "You see, in Dodoland there's a blessed field known to everybody as the Field of Miracles. In this field you dig a little hole and you put, say, a gold piece in it. Then you cover the hole over again with some earth, water it with two bucketsful of spring water, sprinkle a pinch of salt over it, and in the evening you go peacefully to bed. Meanwhile, during the night the gold piece sprouts and blossoms, and as soon as you're up the next morning, you go back to the field and what do you find? You find a beautiful tree laden with as many gold pieces as a good ear of corn has grains in the month of June."

"Why then," said Pinocchio, more amazed than ever, "if I buried my five gold pieces in that field, how many would I find there the next morning?"

"That's easy enough to figure out," answered the Fox, "you can do it on your fingers. Suppose that each gold piece makes a bunch of five hundred; multiply the five hundred by five, and the next morning there you are with two thousand, five hundred shiny, clinking gold pieces in your pocket."

"Oh, how wonderful!" shouted Pinocchio, dancing for joy. "As soon as I've picked the gold pieces I'll keep two thousand for myself, and I'll give the remaining five hundred to you two as a present."

"A present for us?" cried the Fox, taking offense and claiming to be insulted. "Heaven forbid!"

"Forbid!" repeated the Cat.

"We," continued the Fox, "we do not work for miserable personal gain; we work only to enrich others."

"Others!" repeated the Cat.

"What wonderful people!" Pinocchio thought to himself. And forgetting on the spot all about his father, the new jacket, the spelling book, and all the good resolutions he had made, he said to the Fox and the Cat:

"Let's get going! I'm coming with you."

CHAPTER XIII

They arrive at
the Red Crawfish Inn.

hey began to walk and walk and walk and walk, until toward evening they finally arrived dead tired at the Red Crawfish Inn.

"Let's stop here for a while," said the Fox, "just to have a bite to eat and rest for a few hours. Then at midnight we'll start out again, so as to be at the Field of Miracles tomorrow at dawn."

Entering the inn, the three of them sat down at a table, but none of them was hungry.

The poor Cat, suffering from a badly upset stomach, was only able to eat thirty-five red mullets with tomato sauce and four portions of tripe à la Parmesan; and because the tripe didn't seem savory enough, he didn't hesitate to ask for the butter and grated cheese three times.

The Fox also would have been glad to pick at something; but seeing that the doctor had put him on a strict diet, he had to limit himself to hare in sweet-and-sour sauce, meagerly garnished with plump pullets and prime cockerels. After the hare, he ordered a small fricassee of partridges, rabbits, frogs, lizards, and dried sweet paradise grapes. Following this, he took nothing else. He felt such nausea at the thought of food, so he said, that he couldn't bring anything to his mouth.

It was Pinocchio who ate least of all. He asked for a quarter of a walnut and a small piece of bread crust, but he left everything on his plate. With his mind fixed on the Field of Miracles, the poor boy had a case of anticipatory indigestion from gold coins.

After they had supped, the Fox said to the innkeeper: "Let us have two nice rooms, one for Signor Pinocchio and another for me and my companion. Before starting out again we'll squeeze out a few winks. But remember that at midnight we want to be awakened so we can continue our journey."

"Yessir," replied the innkeeper, and he winked at the Fox and the Cat, as if to say: "I get it, and you can count on me."

As soon as Pinocchio got into bed, he fell right to sleep and began to dream. In his dream he saw himself in the middle of a field; the field was full of small trees laden with clusters, and the clusters were laden with gold pieces that went clinkety-clink while swaying in the wind, as if to say: "Whoever wants us, come and get us." But just when Pinocchio was at the best part, that is, when he stretched out his hands to take fistfuls of those beautiful coins and put them in his pocket, he was rudely awakened by three loud knocks on the door of his room.

It was the innkeeper, who had come to tell him that midnight had struck.

"And are my companions ready?" the puppet asked him.

"I'll say they're ready! They left two hours ago."

"Why in such a hurry?"

"Because the Cat received a message saying that his eldest kitten, suffering from chilblains, was near death."

"Did they pay for the supper?"

"How can you think that? They are too well bred to insult your lordship like that!"

"What a pity! I would have been glad to receive such an insult!" said Pinocchio, scratching his head. Then he asked:

"And where did those good friends of mine say they would wait for me?"

"In the Field of Miracles, at the crack of dawn."

Pinocchio paid a gold piece for his supper and for that of his companions, and then went on his way.

But you can say that he went gropingly, because outside the inn it was dark, so dark that it was impossible to see a step ahead. All around in the countryside not even a leaf was heard rustling. Only a few scary night birds, crossing the road now and then from one hedge to the other, hit their wings against Pinocchio's nose. Jumping back in fright, he shouted: "Who goes there!" And in the distance the echo from the surrounding hills repeated: "Who goes there? Who goes there? Who goes there?"

In the meantime, as he walked on, he saw a tiny creature on the trunk of a tree, glowing with a dim and pale light, like a night candle inside a transparent china lamp.

"Who are you?" Pinocchio asked.

"I am the ghost of the Talking Cricket," answered the tiny creature, in a faint little voice that seemed to come from the world beyond.

"What do you want with me?" said the puppet.

"I want to give you a piece of advice. Go back and take the four gold pieces you still have left to your poor father, who is weeping in despair at not seeing you anymore."

"Tomorrow my father will be a wealthy man, because these four gold pieces are going to become two thousand."

"My boy, don't trust people who promise to make you rich overnight. Usually, they are either madmen or swindlers. Listen to me; go back."

"I want to go on."

"The hour is late!"

"I want to go on."

"The night is dark...."

"I want to go on."

"The way is dangerous...."

"I want to go on."

"Remember that children who want their own way regret it sooner or later."

"The same old story. Good night, Cricket."

"Good night, Pinocchio, and may heaven protect you from the dampness and the assassins."

No sooner had he spoken these last words than the Talking Cricket suddenly went out, as a candle goes out when you blow on it, and the road was left darker than before.

CHAPTER XIV

For not listening to the good advice of the Talking Cricket, Pinocchio runs into the assassins.

"**R**eally," said the puppet to himself, resuming his journey, "how unlucky we poor boys are! Everybody scolds us, everybody criticizes us, everybody gives us advice. If they had their way, they'd all take it into their heads to be our fathers and teachers, all of them, even Talking Crickets. Now, for example, just because I wouldn't listen to that gloomy Cricket, who knows, according to him, how many disasters must befall me. I'm even supposed to run into assassins! It's a good thing I don't believe in assassins; and I never have believed in them either. As far as I'm concerned, assassins were invented on purpose by fathers just to frighten children who want to go out at night. And besides, even if I happened to meet them here on the road, do you think they'd scare me? Not in the least. I'd go right up to them and shout: 'You assassins there, what do you want with me? Take heed that I'm not to be trifled with. So go on about your business, and shush!' I can just see those poor assassins rush off like the wind at such sharp talk. But if they happened to be so ill-mannered as not to run off, then I'd run away, and that would be the end of that!"

But Pinocchio wasn't able to finish his discourse, because just then he thought he heard a slight rustling of leaves behind him.

He turned around to look, and there, in the darkness, he saw two horrid black shapes, all loosely wrapped in charcoal sacks. They were chasing after him in leaps on tiptoe, like two ghosts.

"They're really here!" he said to himself; and not knowing where to hide his four gold pieces, he put them in his mouth, right under his tongue.

Then he tried to run away. But he hadn't yet taken the first step when he felt himself grabbed by the arms and heard two horrible, deep voices saying to him:

"Your money or your life!"

Unable to reply in words because of the coins he had in his mouth, Pinocchio made a thousand bows and gestures, trying to convince those two shrouded figures, whose eyes alone could be seen through the holes in the

54

sacks, that he was just a poor puppet and that he didn't have so much as a bad penny in his pocket.

"Come on! Less blab, and out with your money!" the two brigands cried threateningly.

But the puppet made a sign with his head and hands as if to say: "I don't have any."

"Hand over your money or you're a dead man!" said the taller of the two assassins.

"A dead man!" replied the other.

"And after we've killed you, we'll kill your father, too."

"Your father, too!"

"No, no, no, not my poor father!" cried Pinocchio in an anguished voice; but in crying out like that, the gold pieces clinked in his mouth.

"Aha, you scoundrel! So you've hidden the money under your tongue. Spit it out, right away!"

But Pinocchio stood firm.

"Ah! So you're playing deaf, are you? Just wait a moment, we'll get you to spit it out."

With that, one of them gripped the puppet by the end of his nose and the other seized him by the chin; then they began to tug rudely, one down and the other up, trying to force him to open his mouth. But no way. It was as if the puppet's mouth had been nailed and riveted.

Then the shorter assassin pulled out a horrid knife and tried to stick it between the puppet's lips like a lever or a chisel; but Pinocchio, as quick as a flash, dug his teeth into his hand, and after biting it clean off, he spat it out. Imagine his astonishment when he realized that instead of a hand he had spat a cat's paw to the ground.

Taking heart at this initial victory, he struggled free from the claws of the assassins, and jumping over the hedge by the roadside, he began to flee across the fields—with the assassins after him like two dogs pursuing a hare. The one who had lost a paw ran on one leg alone, and nobody ever knew how he managed it.

After a race of fifteen miles, Pinocchio was worn out. Then, out of desperation, he scrambled up the trunk of a very tall pine tree and settled down in the topmost branches. The assassins tried to climb up, too, but when they got halfway up the trunk, they slipped and fell back to the ground, badly scraping their hands and feet.

Despite that, they didn't give up; in fact, after gathering a bundle of dry sticks at the foot of the pine, they set fire to it. In no time at all the tree took fire and began to blaze like a candle in the wind. Seeing the flames rising higher and higher, and not wanting to end up like a roasted pigeon, Pinocchio made a great leap from the top of the tree, and away he ran again across fields and vineyards— and the assassins ran behind him, always giving chase, without ever tiring.

Meanwhile day was beginning to break, and the chase was still on, when suddenly Pinocchio found his way blocked by a wide and very deep ditch, full of filthy water, brownish in color. What to do? "One, two, three!" cried the puppet, and taking a running start he vaulted to the other bank. The assassins jumped too, but having misjudged the distance, splash!...they fell right into the middle of the ditch. Pinocchio, who heard the plunge and the splashing of water, cried out with laughter, running all the time:

"Have a nice bath, my dear assassins."

He was already thinking that they were good and drowned when, turning around to look, he saw instead that they were both running after him, still wrapped in their sacks and streaming with water like two bottomless baskets.

CHAPTER XV

The assassins pursue Pinocchio, and after catching him they hang him from a branch of the Great Oak tree.

Having lost heart now, the puppet was just about to throw himself to the ground and give up when, looking around through the midst of the dark green of the trees, he saw a little house as white as snow gleaming in the distance.

"If only I had enough breath to reach that house, maybe I'd be saved," he said to himself.

And without hesitating a minute, he resumed running through the forest at full speed, the assassins still right behind him.

And after a wild chase of almost two hours, gasping for breath, he finally reached the door of that little house and knocked.

Nobody answered.

He knocked again, harder, because he could hear his tormentors' footsteps nearing and their heavy labored breath. The same silence.

Realizing that knocking did no good, in desperation he began to kick the door and bang his head against it. Then there came to the window a beautiful Little Girl with blue hair and a face as white as a wax image who, with eyes closed and hands crossed over her breast, without moving her lips at all, said in a voice that seemed to come from the world beyond:

"There is nobody in this house. They are all dead."

"Well, then you at least open up for me!" cried Pinocchio, weeping and imploring.

"I am dead, too."

"Dead? But then what are you doing there at the window?"

"I am waiting for the bier to come and take me away."

As soon as she said this, the Little Girl disappeared, and the window closed again without making a sound.

"O beautiful Little Girl with blue hair," cried Pinocchio, "open for me, for mercy's sake. Have pity on a poor boy chased by assass—"

But he was unable to finish the word, because he felt himself being grasped by the neck and heard the same two terrible voices that growled threateningly at him:

"Now you won't get away from us again."

Seeing death flash before his eyes, the puppet was seized by such a violent fit of trembling that the joints of his wooden legs and the four gold coins hidden under his tongue resounded.

"Well then?" the assassins asked him. "Will you open your mouth, yes or no? Ah, you won't answer? It doesn't matter, because this time we'll make you open it."

And drawing out two very long horrible knives sharpened like razors, zack zack, they let him have two blows in the small of the back.

But to the puppet's good fortune he was made of such extremely hard wood that the blades snapped and splintered into a thousand pieces, and the assassins were left with the knife handles in their hands, looking into one another's faces.

"I get it," said one of them then: "We have to hang him. Let's hang him!"

"Let's hang him!" repeated the other.

Without further ado they tied his hands behind his back; and after passing a slip noose around his neck they strung him up to the branch of a big tree called the Great Oak.

Then they settled down there on the grass, waiting for the puppet to kick his last; but after three hours the puppet had his eyes open, his mouth shut, and he was kicking harder than ever.

At last, tired of waiting, they turned to Pinocchio, and laughing sarcastically they said to him:

"Good-bye until tomorrow. When we come back here tomorrow we hope that you'll do us the courtesy of letting yourself be found good and dead, and with your mouth wide open."

And they went away.

Meanwhile a strong north wind had come up, which, blowing and howling furiously, slammed the poor hanged puppet back and forth, causing him to swing violently like the clapper of a joyously ringing bell. And that swinging caused him the sharpest spasms while the slip noose, tightening more and more around his throat, was choking him.

Little by little his eyes grew dim; and although he felt death approaching, he nonetheless still continued to hope that at any moment some compassionate soul would pass by and help him. But when, after waiting and waiting, he saw that nobody showed up, absolutely nobody, then he remembered his poor father again...and almost at death's door, he stuttered:

"Oh, dear father!... If only you were here!"

And he had no breath to say anything else. He closed his eyes, opened his mouth, stretched out his legs, and, after giving a great shudder, he remained there as though frozen stiff.

CHAPTER XVI

The beautiful Little Girl with blue hair has the puppet taken down; she puts him to bed and calls in three doctors to learn whether he is dead or alive.

hile poor Pinocchio, strung up by the assassins to a branch of the Great Oak, by now seemed more dead than alive, the beautiful Little Girl with blue hair came to the window again; and being moved to pity at the sight of the poor wretch, who, as he dangled by the neck was dancing a jig to the gusts of the north wind, she struck her hands together three times and made three faint claps.

At this signal was heard a loud whir of wings in precipitate flight, and a large Falcon came and perched on the windowsill.

"What is your command, my gracious Fairy?" said the Falcon, lowering his beak in a sign of reverence (because you should know, after all, that the Little Girl with blue hair was nothing other than a good Fairy who for more than a thousand years had been living near that forest).

"Do you see that puppet hanging from a branch of the Great Oak?"

"I see him."

"Now then, fly swiftly there; with your strong beak break the knot that holds him suspended in the air, and gently lay him on the grass at the foot of the Oak."

The Falcon flew off and in two minutes returned, saying:

"What you have commanded me is done."

"And how did you find him? Dead or alive?"

"To look at him, he seemed dead; but he probably isn't quite dead yet, because as soon as I undid the noose that was choking him, he let out a sigh and murmured: 'I feel better now.'"

Striking her hands, the Fairy then made two faint claps and there appeared a magnificent Poodle who walked upright on his hind legs, just exactly as if he were a man.

The Poodle was dressed as a coachman in his finest livery. He wore a gold-braided three-cornered hat on his head, a white wig with curls that came down to his neck, a chocolate-colored jacket with diamond buttons and two large pockets to hold the bones that his mistress gave him at dinner, a pair of crimson velvet breeches, silk stockings, pumps, and a sort of umbrella case made of blue satin, to put his tail into when it began to rain.

"Quick, my good Medoro," said the Fairy to the Poodle. "Harness the most beautiful carriage in my coachhouse and take the forest road. When you arrive under the Great Oak, you will find a poor puppet stretched out half dead on the grass. Pick him up gently, lay him with care on the cushions in the carriage, and bring him here to me. Do you understand?"

The Poodle, to show that he had understood, wagged the deep-blue satin case he had behind him three or four times and set off like a racehorse.

In a little while, out of the coachhouse came a beautiful little carriage the color of air, all padded with canary feathers, and lined on the inside with whipped cream and ladyfingers in custard. The carriage was drawn by a hundred pairs of white mice, and the Poodle, sitting on the box, cracked his whip left and right, like a driver who is afraid of being late.

A quarter of an hour hadn't yet gone by when the little carriage

returned. Then the Fairy, who was waiting at the door of the house, took the poor puppet in her arms; and after carrying him into a little room that had mother-of-pearl walls, she immediately sent for the most distinguished doctors in the neighborhood.

And the doctors arrived quickly, one after the other: that is, there arrived a Raven, an Owl, and a Talking Cricket.

"I want to know from you gentlemen," said the Fairy, addressing the three doctors gathered around Pinocchio's bed, "I want to know from you gentlemen whether this unfortunate puppet is dead or alive."

At this invitation the Raven, coming forward first, felt Pinocchio's

pulse, then he felt his nose, then the little toe of each foot; and when he had felt all over thoroughly, he solemnly pronounced these words:

"In my opinion, the puppet is good and dead; but if, by some misfortune, he should not be dead, then it would be a sure indication that he is still alive."

"I am sorry," said the Owl, "to have to contradict my illustrious friend and colleague, the Raven. For me, on the contrary, the puppet is still alive; but if, by some misfortune, he should not be alive, then it would be an indication that he is indeed dead."

"And have you nothing to say?" the Fairy asked the Talking Cricket.

"I say that the best thing the prudent doctor can do when he doesn't know what he's talking about is to keep quiet. Besides, that puppet's face is not new to me, I have known him for some time."

Pinocchio, who until then had been motionless like a true piece of wood, was seized with a kind of convulsive shudder that made the whole bed shake.

"That puppet there," continued the Talking Cricket, "is a confirmed rascal."

Pinocchio opened his eyes and closed them again quickly.

"He's a nasty urchin, a loafer, a vagabond...."

Pinocchio hid his face under the sheets.

"That puppet there is a disobedient child who will make his poor father die of heartbreak."

At this point, there was heard in the room a stifled sound of crying and sobbing. Imagine how surprised they all were when, upon lifting the sheets up a little, they discovered that it was Pinocchio who was crying and sobbing.

"When the deceased cries, it is an indication that he is on the road to recovery," said the Raven solemnly.

"It grieves me to contradict my illustrious friend and colleague," added the Owl, "but for me, when the deceased cries, it is an indication that he is sorry to die."

CHAPTER XVII

Pinocchio eats the sugar, but refuses
to swallow his medicine; however, when he
sees the undertakers coming to take him away,
he swallows the medicine. Then he
tells a lie, and as a punishment
his nose grows longer.

s soon as the three doctors had left the room, the Fairy came up to Pinocchio; and when she touched him on the forehead, she realized that he was running an incredibly high fever.

So she dissolved a certain fine white powder in half a glass of water, and handing it to the puppet she said tenderly:

"Drink it, and in a few days you will be better."

Pinocchio looked at the glass, made a wry face, and then asked in a whining voice:

"Is it sweet or bitter?"

"It's bitter, but it will do you good."

"If it's bitter, I don't want it."

"Listen to me. Drink it."

"I don't like bitter things."

"Drink it; and after you have drunk it, I'll give you a lump of sugar to take away the taste."

"Where's the lump of sugar?"

"Here it is," said the Fairy, taking it out of a gold sugar bowl.

"First I want the lump of sugar, and then I'll drink that awful, bitter stuff."

"Is that a promise?"

"Yes."

The Fairy gave him the sugar lump and, after crunching and swallowing it down in a flash, Pinocchio said, licking his lips:

"How wonderful it would be if sugar were also medicine! I'd take it every day."

"Now keep your promise and drink these few drops of water that will make you well again."

Pinocchio took the glass in his hands reluctantly and stuck the tip of his nose in it; then he brought it to his lips; then he put the tip of his nose in it again; finally he said:

"It's too too bitter! I can't drink it."

"How can you tell, if you haven't even tried it?"

"I can tell because I've smelled it! First I want another lump of sugar...and then I'll drink it."

So the Fairy, with all the patience of a good mother, put another bit of sugar into his mouth, after which she handed him the glass again.

"I can't drink it this way," said the puppet, making all kinds of faces.

"Why not?"

"Because that cushion there on my feet bothers me."

The Fairy took away the cushion.

"It's no use! Even like that, I can't drink it."

"What else bothers you?"

"The door of the room, which is half open, bothers me."

The Fairy got up and closed the door.

"The fact is," cried Pinocchio, bursting into tears, "I don't want to drink that awful bitter stuff. I won't, I won't, I won't."

"My boy, you'll be sorry."

"I don't care."

"You are seriously ill."

"I don't care."

"The fever will carry you off to the next world in a few short hours."

"I don't care."

"Aren't you afraid of dying?"

"Not in the least afraid! Better to die than drink that terrible medicine."

At that very moment the door of the room opened wide and in came four rabbits as black as ink, carrying a small coffin on their shoulders.

"What do you want from me?" cried Pinocchio, sitting up straight in terror.

"We have come to get you," replied the biggest rabbit.

"To get me? But I'm not dead yet!"

"Not yet; but you have only a few minutes of life left, since you refused to drink the medicine that would have cured you of the fever."

"O my Fairy, my Fairy," the puppet then began to scream, "give me the glass right away. Hurry, for heaven's sake; I don't want to die, no, I don't want to die!"

And clutching the glass with both hands, he emptied it in one gulp.

"Well, so much for that!" said the rabbits. "We've made the trip for nothing this time." And lifting the little coffin up on their shoulders again, they went out of the room, snorting and muttering under their breath.

The fact is that in a few minutes Pinocchio hopped out of bed, all better; because, you see, wooden puppets have the privilege of rarely getting sick and of getting better very quickly.

And the Fairy, seeing him run and romp around the room as brisk and cheerful as a cockerel just beginning to crow, said to him:

"So then my medicine really did you some good?"

"More than good! It brought me back to life."

"Then why did you have to be begged so much to drink it?"

"It's just that we boys are all like that. We're more afraid of medicine than of being sick."

"Shame on you! Children should know that a good medicine taken in time can save them from a serious illness and perhaps even from death."

"Oh, but the next time I won't make such a fuss. I'll remember those black rabbits with the coffin on their shoulders...and then I'll take the glass in my hands right away, and down it'll go!"

"Now come over here to me and tell me how it happened that you came into the hands of the assassins."

"What happened was that Fire-Eater the puppeteer gave me some gold coins and said: 'Here, take these to your father,' but instead I met a Fox and a Cat on the way, two very nice people, who said: 'Do you want those five coins to turn into a thousand or even two thousand? Come with us, and we'll take you to the Field of Miracles.' So I said: 'Let's go'; and they said: 'Let's stop here at the Red Crawfish Inn, and after midnight we'll go on again.' But then, when I woke up, they weren't there any more, because they had left. So then I began to make my way at night where it was so dark you wouldn't believe it, so that on the way I met two assassins inside two charcoal sacks, who said to me: 'Hand over your money,' and I said to them: 'I don't have any,' because those four gold coins, well, I had hidden them in my mouth, so one of the assassins tried to get his hands in my mouth, so I bit his hand off and spat it out, but instead of a hand I spat out a cat's paw. And the assassins were chasing after me while I was running with all my might to stay ahead of them until they caught me and tied me by the neck to a tree in this forest, saying: 'Tomorrow we'll come back here, and then you'll be dead with your mouth open, and that way we'll take away the gold coins that you've hidden under your tongue.'"

"And now where have you put the four coins?" the Fairy asked him.

"I've lost them," replied Pinocchio; but he was telling a lie, because in fact he had them in his pocket.

As soon as he had told the lie, his nose, which was already rather long, immediately grew another two inches.

"And where did you lose them?"

"In the forest nearby."

At this second lie, his nose grew still more.

"If you lost them in the forest nearby," said the Fairy, "we'll look for them and find them again; because everything that is lost in the nearby forest is always found again."

"Ah, now that I think of it," replied the puppet, getting confused, "I didn't lose the four coins, but without realizing it I swallowed them while I was drinking your medicine."

At this third lie, his nose grew so extraordinarily long that poor Pinocchio could no longer turn around. If he turned this way he bumped his nose against the bed or the windowpanes; if he turned that way, he bumped it against the wall or the door of the room; if he raised his head a little, he ran the risk of poking it into one of the Fairy's eyes.

And the Fairy looked at him and laughed.

"Why are you laughing?" the puppet asked her, quite embarrassed and worried about that nose of his that was growing before his very eyes.

"I'm laughing at the lie you told."

"How do you know that I've told a lie?"

"Lies, my dear boy, are quickly discovered; because there are two kinds. There are lies with short legs, and lies with long noses. Yours is clearly of the long-nosed variety."

Pinocchio, not knowing where to hide himself for shame, tried to run from the room; but he couldn't. His nose had grown so much that it could no longer pass through the door.

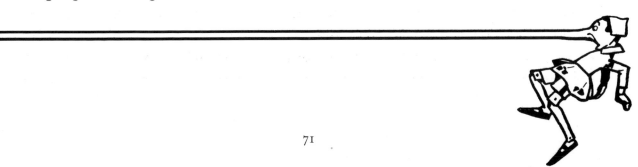

CHAPTER XVIII

Pinocchio comes across the Fox and the Cat again and goes with them to sow the four coins in the Field of Miracles.

s you can well imagine, the Fairy let the puppet cry and yell for a good half hour over that nose of his that could no longer get through the door of the room; and she did it to give him a severe lesson so that he would rid himself of the ugly habit of telling lies, the worst fault a boy can have. But when she saw him disfigured and with his eyes popping out of his head in wild despair, she was moved to pity and clapped her hands; and at that signal, in through the window came about a thousand large birds called woodpeckers who perched on Pinocchio's nose and set about pecking at it in such good measure that in a few minutes that huge, exaggerated nose was brought back to its natural size.

"How good you are, my Fairy," said the puppet, drying his eyes, "and how much I love you!"

"I love you too," replied the Fairy, "and if you want to stay with me, you shall be my little brother, and I your good little sister."

"I'd be glad to stay...but my poor father?"

"I have thought of everything. Your father has already been told, and before nightfall he'll be here."

"Really?" cried Pinocchio, jumping with joy. "Then, my dear little Fairy, if it's all right with you, I would like to go and meet him on the way. I can't wait to kiss that poor old man who has suffered so much on my account."

"Go ahead, but be sure not to go astray. Take the forest path, and I'm sure that you will meet him."

Pinocchio set out, and as soon as he entered the forest, he started to run like a deer. But when he came to a certain spot, almost in front of the Great Oak, he stopped, because he thought he heard someone amid the foliage. In fact, he saw appear on the road—guess who?—the Fox and the Cat, that is, the two traveling companions with whom he had supped at the Red Crawfish Inn.

"Here's our dear Pinocchio!" cried the Fox, embracing and kissing him. "How do you happen to be here?"

"How do you happen to be here?" repeated the Cat.

"It's a long story," said the puppet, "and I'll tell you about it when it's more convenient. But I can tell you now that the other night, after you left me alone at the inn, I met the assassins on the road."

"The assassins? Oh, my poor friend! But what did they want?"

"They wanted to steal my gold coins."

"Villains!" said the Fox.

"Villainous villains!" repeated the Cat.

"But I began to run," the puppet went on, "and they kept after me until they caught me and hanged me from a branch of that oak tree."

And Pinocchio pointed to the Great Oak, which was right close by.

"Have you ever heard anything so awful!" said the Fox. "What a world we are condemned to live in! Is there no haven for honest men such as we?"

While they were talking in this way, Pinocchio noticed that the Cat limped on his right foreleg, because his whole paw, claws and all, was missing from the end of it; so he asked him:

"What have you done with your paw?"

The Cat tried to answer something, but became confused. So then the Fox said quickly:

"My friend is too modest, and that's why he doesn't answer. I will answer for him. You see, an hour ago on the road we met an old wolf, nearly fainting from hunger, who begged us for alms. Not having so much as a fishbone to give him, what did my friend, who truly has the heart of a Caesar, do? With his own teeth he bit off a paw from one of his forelegs and cast it to the poor beast so that he might break his fast."

And in relating this, the Fox wiped away a tear.

Pinocchio, who was also moved, went up to the Cat, whispering in his ear:

"If all cats were like you, how lucky the mice would be!"

"But now what are you doing in these parts?" the Fox asked the puppet.

"I'm waiting for my father who should be coming by at any moment."

"And your gold coins?"

"I still have them in my pocket, except one that I spent at the Red Crawfish Inn."

"And to think that instead of four coins, tomorrow they could be a thousand or even two thousand! Why don't you listen to my advice? Why don't you go and sow them in the Field of Miracles?"

"Today it's impossible; I'll go there another day."

"Another day will be too late," said the Fox.

"Why?"

"Because the field has been bought by a rich gentleman, and beginning tomorrow nobody will be allowed to sow money there."

"How far is the Field of Miracles from here?"

"Hardly two miles. Do you want to come with us? In half an hour you're there, you sow the four coins right away, after a few minutes you gather two thousand of them, and this evening you return here with your pockets full. Do you want to come with us?"

Pinocchio hesitated a little before answering, because he thought of the good Fairy, old Geppetto, and the warnings of the Talking Cricket; but then he ended by doing what all boys do who haven't a shred of sense and are heartless: that is, he ended by shrugging his shoulders and saying to the Fox and the Cat:

"Let's go; I'm coming with you."

And they went on their way.

After walking for half a day, they came to a town called Catchafool. As soon as he entered the town, Pinocchio saw all the streets crowded with mangy dogs yawning with hunger, fleeced sheep shivering with cold, hens bereft of crest and wattle begging for a kernel of corn, large butterflies no longer able to fly because they had sold their beautiful colored wings, tailless peacocks ashamed to be seen, and pheasants who waddled about silently, mourning their brilliant feathers of gold and silver lost forevermore.

In the midst of this crowd of beggars and downcast poor, from time to time an elegant carriage would pass by, with either a fox or a thieving magpie, or a horrid bird of prey inside.

"But where is the Field of Miracles?" asked Pinocchio.

"It's right nearby here."

Without further ado, they crossed the city, and going out beyond the walls they stopped in an isolated field that looked more or less like any other field.

"And here we are," said the Fox to the puppet. "Now stoop to the ground, dig a little hole in the field with your hands, and put the gold coins in it."

Pinocchio obeyed; he dug the hole, put his remaining four gold coins inside, and then covered the hole over again with some earth.

"Now, then," said the Fox, "go to the nearby ditch, get a bucket of water, and sprinkle the ground where you sowed."

Pinocchio went to the ditch and since he didn't have a bucket on hand just then, he took off one of his clogs, and after filling it with water he sprinkled the earth that covered the hole. Then he asked:

"Is there anything else to be done?"

"Nothing else," replied the Fox. "We can go away now. Then you come back here in about twenty minutes, and you'll find the little tree has already come up through the soil, with its branches all laden with coins."

The poor puppet, beside himself with joy, thanked the Fox and the Cat a thousand times and promised them a beautiful gift.

"We do not desire gifts," replied those two rogues. "It's enough for us to have taught you how to become rich without effort, and for that we are as happy as a holiday."

So saying, they bade farewell to Pinocchio, and wishing him a rich harvest they went off about their business.

Pinocchio is robbed of his gold coins, and as a punishment he gets four months in prison.

aving returned to the city, the puppet began to count the minutes one by one, and when he thought it was time, he quickly went back to the road that led to the Field of Miracles.

And as he hurried along his heart was beating fast and going tick-tock, tick-tock, like a grandfather clock when it's really running strong. Meanwhile he thought to himself:

"And if instead of a thousand coins, I found two thousand in the branches of the tree? And if instead of two thousand I found five thousand? And if instead of five thousand I found a hundred thousand? Oh! What a wealthy gentleman I'd become then! I'd get myself a beautiful palace, a thousand little wooden horses and a thousand stables to play with, a cellar full of cordials and liqueurs, and a library chock-full of candied fruit, pies, almond cakes, and rolled wafers filled with whipped cream."

While he was building these castles in the air, he came near the field and stopped to see if by chance he could make out a tree with its branches laden with coins; but he didn't see anything. He went ahead another hundred steps: still nothing. He entered the field, went right up to the little hole where he had buried his gold pieces: still nothing. Then he became worried; and forgetting all the rules of etiquette and good manners, he took his hand out of his pocket and stood there scratching his head for a long time.

Suddenly a great screech of laughter pierced his ears; and looking up he saw a large Parrot in a tree, pecking the fleas from the few feathers he still had on him.

"What are you laughing at?" Pinocchio asked, peevishly.

"I'm laughing because in pecking the fleas from my feathers I tickled myself under my wings."

The puppet said nothing. He went to the ditch and after filling that same clog of his with water set about once more to sprinkle the earth that covered his gold coins.

But then—another burst of laughter, even more impudent than the first, resounded in the deep silence of that lonely field.

"All right, then," shouted Pinocchio, getting quite angry, "may I know, ill-bred Parrot, what you are laughing at?"

"I'm laughing at those dodoes who believe all kinds of nonsense and let themselves be tricked by anyone who is more cunning than they are."

"Are you speaking of me, by any chance?"

"Yes, I'm speaking of you, poor Pinocchio, of you who are so lacking in salt as to believe that money can be sown and harvested in the fields, like beans and pumpkins. There was a time when I believed that too, but I'm paying for it now. Now (when it's too late!) I've come to realize that in order to put together a little money honestly, we must know how to earn it with the labor of our own hands or the wit of our own brains."

"I don't know what you mean," said the puppet, who was already beginning to tremble with fear.

"All right! I'll explain myself better," continued the Parrot. "You see, while you were in town the Fox and the Cat came back to this field, took the

gold coins buried here and then fled like the wind. And whoever catches up with them now will be quite a fellow."

Pinocchio stood there with his mouth open; and not wanting to believe the Parrot's words, with his hands and nails he began to dig up the ground he had watered. And—dig, dig, dig,—he made such a deep hole that a haystack would have fit upright in it; but the coins were no longer there.

Seized with panic then, he rushed back to town and went straight to the court house to denounce the two brigands before the judge.

The judge was a big ape of the gorilla family, elderly and venerable for his advanced years and his white beard, but above all for his gold-rimmed spectacles without lenses, which he was obliged to wear all the time on account of an inflammation of the eyes that had been plaguing him for many years.

Before the judge, Pinocchio recounted in great detail the events of the iniquitous fraud of which he had been the victim; he gave the first names, the surnames, and a description of the brigands, and then finished by asking for justice.

The judge listened to him very sympathetically, took a keen interest in the tale, was touched and deeply moved, and when the puppet had nothing else to say he stretched out his hand and rang a bell.

At that loud ringing, two mastiffs quickly appeared, dressed as gendarmes.

Then the judge, pointing out Pinocchio to the gendarmes, said:

"This poor devil has been robbed of four gold coins; so seize him and put him in prison right away."

Hearing himself sentenced this way, like a bolt out of the blue, the puppet was dumbfounded and wanted to protest; but the gendarmes, so as not to waste time needlessly, stopped his mouth up and led him away to the clink.

And there he stayed for four months, four long, long months; and he would have remained there even longer had not something quite fortunate occurred. For you must know that the young Emperor who reigned over the town of Catchafool, having won a splendid victory over his enemies, ordered great public rejoicing with illuminations, fireworks, and horse and cycle races; and, as a token of the greatest jubilation, he ordered that the prisons also be opened and all the rogues set free.

"If the others are getting out of prison, I want to go out too," said Pinocchio to the jailer.

"Not you," replied the jailer, "because you're not one of the select company."

"I beg your pardon," Pinocchio retorted; "I'm a rogue too."

"In that case, you are absolutely right," said the jailer; and removing his cap respectfully while bowing to him, he opened the prison gates for him and let him run away.

CHAPTER XX

Freed from prison, Pinocchio sets out to return to the Fairy's house; but along the way he meets a horrible Serpent and then gets caught in an animal trap.

Imagine Pinocchio's joy when he felt himself free. Without the slightest hesitation he rapidly left the town and again took the road that should have led him back to the Fairy's house.

But because a slight drizzle was falling, the whole road had become knee-deep in mud. But the puppet didn't care about that. Wild to see his father and his little blue-haired sister again, he ran in leaps and bounds like a greyhound; and as he ran, the mud splashed up and bespattered him all the way up to his cap. Meanwhile, he was saying to himself:

"How many bad things have happened to me!...But I deserve them, because I'm a stubborn and willful puppet...and I always want things my own way without listening to those who love me and have a thousand times more sense than I have.... But from now on, I make a resolution to change my ways and become a well-behaved and obedient boy. Besides, by now I've seen only too well that when boys are disobedient they always pay for it and things never turn out right for them.... Who knows if my father has waited for me? I wonder if I'll find him at the Fairy's house? Poor man, it's been so long since I last saw him that I'm dying to hug him over and over, and to smother him with kisses.... And will the Fairy forgive me for the terrible thing I've done to her?... And to think that I received so much attention and loving care from her; to think that if I'm still alive today I owe it to her!... Can there be a more ungrateful and heartless boy than I am?"

While he was saying this, he suddenly stopped in terror and took four steps backward.

What had he seen?

He had seen a large Serpent stretched out across the road. It had green skin, fiery eyes, and a pointed tail that smoked like a chimney stack.

You couldn't imagine the puppet's fear; after retreating more than half a mile he sat down on a small pile of stones and waited for the Serpent to go off for good about his business and leave the way free.

He waited an hour, two hours, three hours. But the Serpent was still there, and even from a distance you could see the red glow of his fiery eyes and the column of smoke that was rising from the pointed end of his tail.

Then Pinocchio, trying to seem brave, approached to within a few steps and, speaking in a soft ingratiating voice, said to the Serpent:

"Excuse me, Signor Serpent, I wonder if you would do me the favor of moving over a little bit, just enough to let me go by?"

It was the same as talking to the wall. Nobody moved.

Then he began again in the same soft voice:

"Consider, Signor Serpent, that I am going home where my father is waiting for me, and that I haven't seen him for such a long time. Is it all right with you, then, if I continue on my way?"

He waited for some sign of an answer to this request, but no answer came. On the contrary, the Serpent, who until then had seemed active and full of life, became motionless and rather stiff. His eyes closed and his tail stopped smoking.

"Can he really be dead?" said Pinocchio, rubbing his hands together with glee. And without wasting any time, he made as if to jump over him so as to get to the other side of the road. But he hadn't yet finished lifting his leg when the Serpent suddenly shot up like a released spring; and as the puppet drew back in terror, he stumbled and fell to the ground.

And in fact, he fell so awkwardly that he landed with his head stuck in the mud and his legs straight up in the air.

At the sight of that upside-down puppet frantically kicking his heels, the Serpent was seized with such a fit of laughter that he laughed and laughed and laughed until, from the strain of too much laughing, he burst a blood vessel in his chest; and then he really died.

Then Pinocchio began to run again, trying to reach the Fairy's house before it turned dark. But on the way, not being able to bear the terrible pangs of hunger, he jumped into a field, intending to pick a few bunches of muscat grapes. Would that he had never done it!

As soon as he reached the vines—crack!—he felt his legs clamped tightly between two sharp irons that made him see all the stars there were in the heavens.

The poor puppet had been caught in a trap set there by some peasants to catch a few large martens that were the scourge of all the chicken coops in the neighborhood.

CHAPTER XXI

Pinocchio is caught by a peasant who forces him to work as a watchdog for his poultry yard.

inocchio, as you can imagine, began to cry, to scream, to plead; but his tears and cries were of no use, because no houses were to be seen anywhere around there, and not a living soul passed by along the road. Meanwhile, night came on.

Partly because of the intense pain caused by the animal trap that was sawing at his shinbones, and partly because of his fear at finding himself alone in the dark in the middle of those fields, the puppet was almost on the verge of fainting, when all of a sudden he saw a Firefly passing by overhead and called out to her:

"Oh, dear little Firefly, would you be so kind as to free me from this torture?"

"Poor little fellow!" replied the Firefly, stopping to look at him with pity. "How did you ever get your legs clamped between those sharp irons?"

"I came into the field to pick a few bunches of these muscat grapes, and…"

"But were the grapes yours?"

"No…"

"Then who taught you to take other people's things?"

"I was hungry…"

"Hunger, my boy, is not a good reason for appropriating what is not ours."

"That's true, that's true," cried Pinocchio in tears, "but the next time I won't do it anymore."

At that moment their conversation was interrupted by a light sound of approaching footsteps. It was the owner of the field, who was coming on tiptoe to see if any of the martens that ate his chickens at night had been caught in the trap he had laid.

His astonishment was quite great when after taking his lantern out from under his overcoat he found that, instead of a marten, a boy had been caught.

"Ah, you little thief!" said the peasant in a rage, "so it's you who steals my hens."

"Not me, not me!" cried Pinocchio, sobbing. "I only came into the field to get a few bunches of grapes."

"Anyone who steals grapes is quite capable of stealing chickens too. Leave it to me! I'll teach you a lesson you'll remember for a long time."

And opening the trap, he grabbed the puppet by the scruff of the neck and carried him bodily all the way home, just as you would carry a little lamb.

When he reached the threshing floor in front of the house, he flung him to the ground and, keeping one foot on his neck, he said:

"It's late now, and I want to go to bed. We'll settle our accounts tomorrow. Meanwhile, since the dog that kept watch for me at night died today, you'll take his place right away. You'll be my watchdog."

Without further ado he slipped a big collar covered with brass spikes around the puppet's neck and tightened it so much that Pinocchio couldn't slip it off by pulling his head through it. A long iron chain was attached to the collar; and the chain was fastened to the wall.

"If it begins to rain tonight," said the peasant, "you can go lie down in that wooden doghouse where there's still the same straw that was my poor dog's bed for four years. And if by ill chance those thieves should come, remember to keep your ears cocked and bark."

After this final warning, the peasant went into the house, securing the door with an enormous bolt, while poor Pinocchio remained crouched on the threshing-floor yard, more dead than alive with cold, hunger, and fear. And from time to time, thrusting his hands furiously inside the collar that squeezed his throat, he would say, weeping:

"It serves me right! Unfortunately, it serves me right! I wanted to be a lazybones, a vagabond; I preferred to listen to bad companions, and that's why fortune continues to hound me. If I had been a proper boy, the way so many others are, if I had been willing to study and work, if I had stayed at home with my poor father, I wouldn't find myself here now in the middle of the country, being a watchdog at a peasant's house. Oh, if only I could be born over again! But it's too late now, and I have to put up with it."

Having given vent to these feelings that came right from his heart, he went into the doghouse and fell asleep.

CHAPTER XXII

Pinocchio catches the thieves, and as a reward for his loyalty he is set free.

He had already been sleeping soundly for more than two hours when, toward midnight, he was awakened by the whispering and low chatter of unfamiliar, soft voices that he thought he heard coming from the threshing floor. Sticking the tip of his nose out of the hole of the doghouse, he saw four small, dark-coated creatures who looked like cats consulting in a huddle. But they were not cats: they were martens, little flesh-eating animals, particularly fond of eggs and plump young chickens. One of these martens, leaving his companions, went up to the hole of the doghouse and said softly:

"Good evening, Melampus."

"My name isn't Melampus," answered the puppet.

"Well, who are you then?"

"I'm Pinocchio."

"And what are you doing there?"

"I'm being the watchdog."

"Well, where's Melampus then? Where's the old dog who used to live in this doghouse?"

"He died this morning."

"He died? Poor creature! He was so good! Still, judging by your looks, you seem to be a pretty decent dog too."

"I beg your pardon; I'm not a dog."

"Well, what are you?"

"I'm a puppet."

"And you're acting as a watchdog?"

"Unfortunately, yes; as a punishment."

"Well then, I'll offer you the same deal that I had with the late Melampus. And you're bound to be satisfied."

"And this deal, what would it be?"

"As in the past, we'll come once a week at night to pay a visit to this chicken coop, and we'll make off with eight hens. Of these hens, we'll eat seven and give one to you on condition, of course, that you pretend to be asleep and never get the notion to bark and wake up the peasant."

"And Melampus really did that?" asked Pinocchio.

"He did; and we always got along well. So sleep peacefully, and rest assured that before going away from here we'll leave you a ready-plucked hen on the doghouse for tomorrow's breakfast. Do we understand each other?"

"Only too well!" replied Pinocchio; and he shook his head in a threatening sort of way, as if to say: "We'll soon see about that."

When the four martens felt sure they had things their way, they went straight to the chicken coop, which was located just by the doghouse; and when by dint of their teeth and claws they had opened the small wooden gate that closed the entranceway, they slipped inside one after the other. But no sooner had they finished going in than they heard the gate slam shut behind them.

It was Pinocchio who had shut it; and not satisfied with just shutting it, he propped a big rock against it as an additional precaution.

Then he began to bark; and barking just as if he really were a watchdog, he made his voice go bow-wow-wow.

At that loud barking the peasant sprang out of bed, and after getting his gun and looking out the window, he asked:

"What's up now?"

"The thieves are here," answered Pinocchio.

"Where are they?"

"In the chicken coop."

"I'll be right down."

And in fact, faster than you can say "Amen," the peasant came down and rushed into the chicken coop; and after seizing the four martens and stuffing them in a sack he said with real satisfaction:

"At last you have fallen into my hands! I could punish you, but I am not that base. Instead, I'll just take you to the innkeeper in the nearby village tomorrow, and he'll skin you and cook you like hare in sweet-and-sour sauce. It's an honor you don't deserve, but magnanimous men like me don't quibble over such trifles."

Then, going up to Pinocchio he began to compliment him enthusiastically, and among other things, he asked him:

"How did you manage to discover the plot of these four petty thieves? And to think that Melampus, my faithful Melampus, never noticed anything!"

The puppet could have told him everything he knew then: that is, he could have told about the shameful pact that existed between the dog and the martens. But remembering that the dog was dead, he immediately thought to himself: "What's the good of accusing the dead? The dead are dead, and the best thing we can do is to leave them in peace."

"When the martens came into the yard, were you awake or were you sleeping?" the peasant went on to ask him.

"I was sleeping," replied Pinocchio, "but the martens woke me up with their chatter; and one of them came right up to the doghouse here to say to me: 'If you promise not to bark and not to wake up the owner, we'll make you a present of a ready-plucked young hen.' Can you imagine, huh? The nerve of making such a proposal to me! Now, you know, I may be a puppet with all the faults in the world, but one fault I'll never have is that of being in cahoots with dishonest people and holding the sack for them!"

"Good for you, my boy!" cried the peasant, slapping him on the back. "Such sentiments do you honor; and to show you how grateful I am, I'm letting you go free right now to return home."

And he removed the dog collar from him.

Pinocchio mourns the death of the beautiful Little Girl with blue hair; then he meets a Pigeon who carries him to the seashore where he leaps into the water to go to the rescue of his father Geppetto.

s soon as Pinocchio no longer felt the heavy and humiliating weight of that dog collar around his neck, he set out on the run across the fields and didn't stop for a single moment until he had reached the main road that should have led him to the Fairy's house.

Once he was on the main road, he turned to look down on the plain below, and with his naked eye he could easily see the forest where, to his misfortune, he had met the Fox and the Cat. There he saw, rising amid the trees, the top of the Great Oak from which he had been left dangling by the neck; but though he looked here, there, and everywhere, he couldn't see the house of the Little Girl with the blue hair.

Then he felt a sort of sad foreboding; and running with all the strength he had left in his legs, in a few minutes he was in the meadow where the little white house once stood. But the little white house was no longer there. Instead, there was a small marble slab on which one could read in block letters these sorrowful words:

HERE LIES

THE LITTLE GIRL WITH THE BLUE HAIR

DEAD WITH GRIEF

FOR HAVING BEEN ABANDONED BY HER

LITTLE BROTHER PINOCCHIO

I leave it to you to imagine how the puppet felt after he had struggled to make out those words. He fell facedown to the ground; and covering the tombstone with a thousand kisses, he burst into a flood of tears. He wept throughout the night, and at daybreak the next morning he was still weeping, although he had no tears left in his eyes. And his cries and wails were so heartrending and piercing that the hills all around resounded with their echo. And weeping, he said:

"Oh, my little Fairy, why did you die? Why didn't I die instead of you, I who am so wicked, while you were so good? And my father, where can he be? Oh, my little Fairy, tell me where I can find him, because I want to stay with him always and never leave him again, never! never! Oh, my little Fairy, tell me it's not true that you're dead! If you really love me, if you love your little brother, live again, come back to life as before! Aren't you sorry to see me alone and abandoned by everyone? If the assassins come, they'll string me up again to the branch of the tree, and then I'll die forever. What can you expect me to do here alone in this world? Now that I have lost you and my father, who will feed me? Where will I go to sleep at night? Who will make me a nice new jacket? Oh, it would be better, a hundred times better, if I died too! Yes, I want to die! Boo-hoo-hoo!"

And while he was wailing in this fashion, he made as if to tear out his hair; but since his hair was of wood, he couldn't even have the satisfaction of thrusting his fingers into it.

At that moment a large Pigeon passed by overhead and, hovering with outspread wings, called out to him from a great height:

"Tell me, child, what are you doing down there?"

"Can't you see? I'm crying!" said Pinocchio, raising his head up toward that voice and rubbing his eyes with the sleeve of his jacket.

"Tell me," the Pigeon added then, "among your comrades, do you by any chance know a puppet named Pinocchio?"

"Pinocchio? Did you say Pinocchio?" the puppet replied, jumping quickly to his feet. "I'm Pinocchio!"

At this answer the Pigeon descended rapidly and alighted on the ground. He was bigger than a turkey.

"Then you probably know Geppetto, too?" he asked the puppet.

"Know him! He's my poor father! Did he speak to you about me? Will you lead me to him? Is he still alive? Answer me, for pity's sake: is he still alive?"

"I left him three days ago on the seashore."

"What was he doing?"

"He was building a little boat by himself, so as to cross the ocean. The poor man, for more than four months he has been going everywhere looking for you; and since he hasn't been able to find you, he has taken it into his head to look for you in the far-off lands of the New World."

"How far is it from here to the shore?" asked Pinocchio in breathless anxiety.

"More than a thousand miles."

"A thousand miles? O dear Pigeon, how wonderful it would be if I had your wings!"

"If you want to go, I'll take you there."

"How?"

"Astride my back. Are you very heavy?"

"Heavy? Quite the contrary! I'm as light as a leaf."

And without another word, Pinocchio jumped on the Pigeon's back and, putting a leg on each side of him the way horsemen do, he shouted happily:

"Gallop, gallop, little horse, for I am eager to get there fast!"

The Pigeon took flight, and in a few minutes he had soared so high that he almost touched the clouds. When he had reached that extraordinary height, the puppet, out of curiosity, turned to look down; but he was seized by so great a fright and such giddiness that, to keep from falling off, he flung his arms as tightly as he could around the neck of his plumed mount.

They flew all day. Toward evening the Pigeon said:

"I'm very thirsty."

"And I'm very hungry," added Pinocchio.

"Let's stop for a few minutes at this dovecote, and then we'll continue our journey so as to be at the seashore by dawn tomorrow."

They went into an empty dovecote where there was nothing but a basin full of water and a basket brimful of vetch.

All his life the puppet had never been able to tolerate vetch. According to him, it nauseated him and turned his stomach; but that evening he ate so much of it that he nearly burst, and when he had almost finished he turned and said to the Pigeon:

"I would never have believed that vetch was so good."

"We have to realize, my boy, that when we are really hungry, and there is nothing else to eat, even vetch can be delicious! Hunger knows neither fancies nor delicacies!"

After a quick snack they set out on their journey again, and away they went! The next morning they arrived at the seashore.

The Pigeon put Pinocchio down, and not wanting to be bothered with hearing himself thanked for having done a good deed, he flew off again at once and disappeared.

The shore was crowded with people yelling and gesticulating as they looked out to sea.

"What's happened?" Pinocchio asked a little old lady.

"What's happened is that a poor father, having lost his child, has insisted on going out in a little boat to look for him beyond the sea; but the waters are very rough today and the boat is about to go under."

"Where's the boat?"

"There it is, out there, in line with my finger," said the old woman, pointing to a small boat that, seen from that distance, looked like a nutshell with a tiny little man in it.

Pinocchio fixed his gaze in that direction and, after looking hard, let out a piercing cry:

"It's my father! It's my father!"

Meanwhile the little boat, tossed about by the fury of the waves, would now disappear amid the large billows and now

94

reappear above them. And Pinocchio, standing on the top of a high rock, never stopped calling his father's name and making him a lot of signs with his hands, his handkerchief, and even with the cap he had on his head.

And although Geppetto was very far from shore, it seemed that he recognized his son, because he too took off his cap and waved at him; and with a flurry of gestures he gave him to understand that he would gladly have come back, but the sea was so rough that it kept him from maneuvering the oars and from being able to approach land.

All of a sudden there was a mighty wave, and the boat disappeared. Everyone waited for it to resurface, but the boat was not seen again.

"Poor man!" said the fishermen then, who were assembled on the shore; and muttering a prayer under their breath, they started to go back home.

But just then they heard a desperate cry, and turning around they saw a little boy jumping from the top of a reef into the sea and shouting:

"I want to save my father!"

Being all of wood, Pinocchio floated easily and swam like a fish. At one moment they saw him disappear under the water, borne down by the rush of the waves, and the next moment he reappeared above with a leg or an arm, at a vast distance from land. Finally, they lost sight of him and saw him no more.

"Poor boy!" said the fishermen then, who were assembled on the shore; and muttering a prayer under their breath, they went home.

CHAPTER XXIV

Pinocchio arrives at the island of Busy Bees and finds the Fairy again.

purred on by the hope of arriving in time to help his poor father, Pinocchio swam the whole night through.

And what an awful night it was! The rain fell in torrents, it hailed, it thundered fearfully, and the lightning was such that it seemed daytime.

Toward morning he was able to see a long strip of land not far off. It was an island in the middle of the sea.

Then he strove with all his might to get to that shore, but in vain. The waves, chasing after one another and tumbling over one another, tossed him all about as if he were a twig or a piece of straw. At last, and a good thing for him, there came a wave so powerful and violent that it dashed him bodily onto the sands of the beach.

He was dashed so hard that in hitting the ground all his ribs and joints cracked; but he quickly consoled himself, saying:

"This time, too, I've had a narrow escape!"

Meanwhile the sky cleared up little by little, the sun came out in all its splendor, and the sea became quite calm and as smooth as oil.

Then the puppet spread his clothes out to dry in the sun and began to look this way and that to see if he could discern on that vast expanse of water a little boat with a little man in it. But although he looked hard and long, he saw nothing in front of him but sky and sea and the occasional sail of a ship, but so very far away that it seemed no bigger than a fly.

"If only I knew the name of this island!" he kept saying. "If only I knew whether this island is inhabited by civilized people; I mean, by people who don't have the bad habit of stringing up boys from tree branches! But who can I possibly ask? Who, if there isn't anybody here?"

The thought of being alone, utterly alone, in the midst of that great uninhabited land put him in such low spirits that he was on the verge of crying. But just then he saw a large fish passing by a little way offshore, going along quietly about his business with all of his head above water.

Not knowing how to call him by name, the puppet called out to him in a loud voice, to make himself heard:

"Ho there, Signor Fish; may I have a word with you?"

"Even two," replied the fish, who was a Dolphin, and so polite that very few of his kind are to be found in all the seas of the world.

"Would you be so kind as to tell me whether there are any villages on this island where one can eat without danger of being eaten?"

"Indeed there are," answered the Dolphin. "In fact, you will find one not far from here."

"And which way do I go to get there?"

"You take that path there on the left and just keep following your nose. You can't go wrong."

"Tell me another thing. You who go through the sea all day and all night, you wouldn't by any chance have come across a small little boat with my father in it?"

"And who is your father?"

"Oh, he's the best father in the world, while I'm the worst son that can be had."

"With the storm we had last night," the Dolphin answered, "the little boat must have gone under."

"And my father?"

"By now he has probably been swallowed by the terrible Whale who has been spreading death and destruction in our waters over the last few days."

"Why, is he very big, this Whale?" asked Pinocchio, who was already beginning to quake with fear.

"Is he big!" replied the Dolphin. "So that you can have an idea of his size, I'll tell you that he is bigger than a five-story building, and has a horrible mouth so wide and deep that a whole railway train with its engine running could easily pass through it."

"Good heavens!" the puppet exclaimed, terrified; and putting his clothes back on in a great hurry he turned to the Dolphin and said:

"Good-bye, Signor Fish; please excuse me for the trouble I've given you, and a thousand thanks for your kindness."

And so saying, he immediately took to the path and began walking at a fast pace—so fast that he seemed almost to be running. And at the slightest sound he heard, he would turn around quickly to look behind him for fear of being pursued by that terrible Whale as big as a five-story building and with a railway train in his mouth.

After half an hour on the road, he came to a small town called Busy-Bee Town. The streets were swarming with people rushing to and fro about their business. Everyone was working; everyone had something to do. Not a single idler or vagabond was to be found, not even if you looked with a lamp for one.

"I see," said that lazybones Pinocchio right away; "this place isn't meant for me. I wasn't born to work."

Meanwhile he was in the throes of hunger, because by now twenty-four hours had gone by without his having eaten anything, not even a dish of vetch.

What was he to do?

There were but two ways left for him to get something in his stomach: either by asking for a little work or by begging for a penny or a piece of bread.

He was ashamed to go begging, because his father had always taught him that only the old and the infirm had a right to ask for charity. The truly poor in this world, those worthy of help and compassion, are only those who by reason of age or infirmity are condemned to being unable to earn their bread with their own hands. Everyone else has the duty of working; and if they don't work and go hungry, so much the worse for them.

At that moment, a man came down the street, perspiring and panting heavily as he struggled to pull two carts full of charcoal by himself.

Judging him by his looks to be a kind man, Pinocchio went up to him, and lowering his eyes for shame, said to him in a low voice:

"Would you be so kind as to give me a penny, because I feel I'm dying of hunger?"

"Not just one penny," replied the coal merchant, "but I'll give you four, provided that you help me to pull home these two carts of charcoal."

"I'm amazed!" answered the puppet, rather indignantly. "I'll have you know that I've never been a jackass. I've never pulled a cart!"

"Good for you," replied the coal merchant. "And so then, my boy, if you're really dying of hunger, eat two good slices of your pride, and watch out that you don't get indigestion."

A few minutes later, a bricklayer passed by carrying a bucket of mortar on his shoulders.

"Good sir, would you be so kind as to give a penny to a poor boy who's yawning with hunger?"

"With pleasure. Come with me to carry mortar," the bricklayer answered, "and instead of one penny I'll give you five."

"But mortar is heavy," replied Pinocchio, "and I don't like hard work."

"If you don't like hard work, my boy, then have fun yawning, and a lot of good may it do you."

In less than half an hour another twenty persons passed by, and Pinocchio begged all of them for a little something, but they all answered:

"Aren't you ashamed of yourself? Instead of hanging around the streets like a loafer, go and look for some work, and learn to earn your bread."

Finally, a kindly woman passed by, carrying two water jugs.

"Kind woman, would you let me have a swallow of water from your jug?" said Pinocchio, who was parched with thirst.

"Go ahead and drink, my boy," said the kindly woman as she set the two jugs on the ground.

After Pinocchio had drunk like a sponge, he mumbled in a low voice while wiping his mouth:

"I've gotten rid of my thirst. If only I could get rid of my hunger now!"

Hearing these words, the kindly woman added quickly:

"If you help me to carry one of these water jugs to my home, I will give you a nice piece of bread."

Pinocchio looked at the jug without answering yes or no.

"And along with the bread, I will give you a nice dish of cauliflower seasoned with oil and vinegar," added the kindly woman.

Pinocchio gave another look at the pitcher, but didn't say yes or no.

"And after the cauliflower, I will give you a nice sugared candy."

The temptation of this last dainty Pinocchio was unable to resist and, his mind made up, he said:

"All right, then! I'll carry the jug home for you."

The jug was very heavy, and since the puppet didn't have enough strength to carry it in his hands, he had to carry it on his head.

After reaching home, the kindly woman sat Pinocchio down at a small table that was already laid and put the bread, the seasoned cauliflower, and the candy before him.

Pinocchio didn't eat; rather he bolted everything down. His stomach was like a lodging that had been left vacant and uninhabited for five months.

Having gradually appeased his violent hunger pangs, he raised his head to thank his benefactress; but he had scarcely looked up into her face when he let out a very long "o-o-o-oh" of surprise, and sat there spellbound, with his eyes wide open, his fork in the air, his mouth full of bread and cauliflower.

"What in the world is all this surprise?" said the kindly woman, laughing.

"It's..." stammered Pinocchio, "it's...it's...just that you resemble...you remind me of...yes, yes, the same voice...the same eyes...the same hair...yes, yes...you have blue hair, too...like her! Oh, my little Fairy, oh, my little Fairy! Tell me that it's you, really you! Don't make me cry anymore! If you only knew! I've cried so much, I've suffered so much!"

As he said this, Pinocchio was shedding floods of tears; and then he fell on his knees to the floor and clasped his arms around the knees of that mysterious woman.

CHAPTER XXV

Pinocchio promises the Fairy that he will be good and go to school, because he is sick and tired of being a puppet and wants to become a good boy.

At first the kindly woman began by saying that she was not the little Fairy with the blue hair, but then, seeing that she had been found out, and not wanting to prolong the game, she finally admitted her identity and said to Pinocchio:

"You scamp of a puppet, how did you ever realize it was I?"

"It's the great love I have for you that told me so."

"Do you remember? When you left me, I was a little girl, and now you find me a woman, such a grown-up woman that I could almost be your mother."

"I'm really glad about that, because now, instead of calling you my little sister, I'll call you my mother. For such a long time now I've yearned to have a mother, like all the other boys…. But how did you manage to grow up so fast?"

"It's a secret."

"Teach it to me; I'd like to grow a little too. Don't you see? I'm still no taller than knee-high to a grasshopper."

"But you can't grow," replied the Fairy.

"Why not?"

"Because puppets never grow. They are born as puppets, they live as puppets, and they die as puppets."

"Oh, I'm sick and tired of always being a puppet!" cried Pinocchio, rapping himself on the head. "It's about time that I too became a man."

"And you will become one, when you learn to deserve it."

"Really? And what can I do to deserve it?"

"Something quite simple: learn how to be a proper boy."

"But isn't that what I already am?"

"Far from it! Proper boys are obedient, and you instead—"

"Instead, I never obey."

"Proper boys are fond of studying and working, you instead—"

"Instead, I'm just a loafer and a vagabond all year round."

"Proper boys always tell the truth—"

"And I tell lies all the time."

"Proper boys are glad to go to school—"

"And school gives me a bellyache. Still, as of today I'm going to turn over a new leaf."

"Do you promise me?"

"I promise. I want to become a proper boy, and I want to be the comfort of my father.... Oh, where can my poor father be now?"

"I don't know."

"Will I ever be lucky enough to see him again and hug him?"

"I think so; in fact, I'm sure of it."

At this answer Pinocchio's joy was so great that he took the Fairy's hands and began to kiss them with such fervor that he seemed beside himself. Then, lifting his face and looking at her lovingly, he asked her:

"Tell me, mother dear, it's not true then that you died?"

"It doesn't seem so," replied the Fairy, smiling.

"If you only knew the grief I felt, and the lump I had in my throat, when I read 'HERE LIES...'"

"I know, and that's why I've forgiven you. The sincerity of your sorrow made me realize that you had a good heart; and there's always something to hope for from boys with good hearts, even if they are a little mischievous and spoiled. That is, there's always the hope that they may mend their ways. That's why I've come all the way here to look for you. I shall be your mother..."

"Oh, how wonderful!" exclaimed Pinocchio, jumping for joy.

"You'll obey me and always do what I tell you."

"I will, I will, I will!"

"As of tomorrow," added the Fairy, "you'll begin to go to school."

At once Pinocchio became a little less elated.

"Then you'll choose a profession or trade to your liking."

Pinocchio became glum.

"What are you muttering under your breath?" asked the Fairy in an irritated tone.

"I was saying..." the puppet whimpered in an undertone, "that it seems a little late for me to start school now...."

"No sir! Bear in mind that it's never too late to study and to learn."

"But I don't want to follow any profession or trade!"

"Why is that?"

"Because work seems like drudgery to me."

"My boy," said the Fairy, "people who talk that way almost always end up in jail or in the poorhouse. Let me tell you that whether one is born rich or poor, one has the duty to do something in this world, to keep busy, to work. Woe to those who yield to idleness! Idleness is a horrible disease, and it has to be cured early, in childhood; otherwise, when we are grown-up, we never get over it."

Pinocchio was very much moved by these words, and lifting his head decisively, he said to the Fairy:

"I'll study, I'll work, I'll do everything you tell me to do, because I'm really fed up with a puppet's life, and I want to become a boy, no matter what. You've promised me, haven't you?"

"I have promised you, and now it's up to you."

CHAPTER XXVI

Pinocchio goes to the seashore with his schoolmates to see the terrible Whale.

he next day Pinocchio went to the public school.

Just imagine those devilish boys when they saw a puppet walk into their school! There was no end of laughter. They played all sorts of tricks on him. One snatched his cap out of his hand, another tugged at his jacket from behind; one of them tried to make a big mustache in ink under his nose, and someone even tried to tie strings to his hands and feet to make him dance.

For a while Pinocchio took it all in stride and didn't pay too much attention to it; but then, feeling his patience was running out, he turned to the ones who were pestering him and making fun of him most and, with a hard look, he said:

"Watch out, fellows; I didn't come here to play the fool for you. I respect others, and I want to be respected."

"Good for you, wise guy! You talk like a printed book!" those little rogues yelled, rolling over with wild laughter. And one who was bolder than the rest stretched out his hand with the intention of grabbing the puppet by the tip of his nose.

But he wasn't quick enough, because Pinocchio thrust his leg under the study bench and gave him a kick in the shins.

"Ouch, what hard feet!" howled the boy, rubbing the bruise that the puppet had caused him.

"And what elbows! Even harder than his feet!" said another, who had got a good poke in the stomach for his rude taunts.

After that kick and that elbow poke, Pinocchio soon won the respect and the affection of all the boys in the school; they all played up to him and were just wild about him.

Even the teacher spoke highly of him, because he saw that he was attentive, studious, and bright, always the first to arrive at school and always the last to get up and leave when school was over.

His one fault was that he went around with too many companions, a good number of whom were urchins well known for their indifference to study and doing well.

PINOCCHIO

His teacher would warn him every day, and the good Fairy too didn't fail to tell him over and over again:

"Be careful, Pinocchio! Sooner or later those good-for-nothing comrades of yours will succeed in making you lose your love for study and may even get you into some serious trouble."

"There's no danger of that!" the puppet would answer, shrugging his shoulders and touching the middle of his forehead with his index finger, as if to say: "There's a lot of good sense in here."

Now it happened that on a certain day while he was walking to school, he met a pack of his usual comrades, who came up to him and said:

"Have you heard the great news?"

"No."

"A Whale as big as a mountain has shown up in the sea not far from here."

"Really? I wonder if it could be the same Whale as the one when my poor father drowned."

"We're going down to the beach to see him. Do you want to come too?"

"Not me! I want to go to school."

"What do you care about school? We'll go to school tomorrow. With one lesson more or less, we'll still be the same jackasses."

"But what will the teacher say?"

"Let the teacher say whatever he likes. He gets paid to grumble all day."

"And my mother?"

"Mothers never know anything," answered those troublemakers.

"Do you know what I'll do?" said Pinocchio, "I have my own good reasons for wanting to see the Whale...but I'll go to see him after school."

"You poor numbskull!" countered one of the gang. "Do you think that a fish as big as that is going to hang around and wait for you? As soon as he gets bored with one place, he makes a beeline for another, and that's the end of that."

"How long does it take from here to the beach?" the puppet asked.

"In an hour we can be there and back."

"Let's go, then! And the first one there is the winner!" shouted Pinocchio.

At this signal to start, that pack of urchins set out on the run across the fields with their textbooks and copybooks under their arms. But Pinocchio kept ahead of them all as though he had wings on his feet.

Once in a while, he turned around to poke fun at his comrades who were far behind; and seeing them gasping for breath, all covered with dust and with their tongues hanging out, he laughed with all his might. The poor wretch little knew at that moment what terrors and horrible misfortunes he was heading toward.

CHAPTER XXVII

There is a great battle between Pinocchio and his comrades, and when one is wounded, Pinocchio is arrested by the carabinieri.

When he got to the beach, Pinocchio immediately gave a sweeping look over the sea, but he saw no Whale. The sea was all smooth, like the surface of a great mirror.

"Well, where's the Whale?" he asked, turning to his comrades.

"He must have gone to have breakfast," answered one of them, laughing.

"Or maybe he hopped into bed to take a nap," added another, laughing still louder.

From their nonsensical answers and their silly jeers, Pinocchio realized that his comrades had played a mean trick on him in giving him to understand something that wasn't true; and taking offense, he said in an irritated voice:

"Well, then? What good did you get out of making me believe that humbug about the Whale?"

"A lot of good, that's for sure!" those rascals answered in a chorus.

"And what would it be?"

"Making you miss school and come with us. Aren't you ashamed of appearing so well prepared and so conscientious every day in class? Aren't you ashamed of studying so hard, the way you do?"

"And what does it matter to you if I study?"

"It matters a whole lot to us, because you make us look bad in front of the teacher."

"Why?"

"Because pupils who study hard always make those of us who don't like to study look bad. And we don't want to look bad. We have our pride too."

"And so what am I supposed to do to please you?"

"You too have got to hate school, and lessons, and the teacher: our three great enemies."

"And what if I want to go on studying?"

"We won't even look at you again, and we'll make you pay for it at the first chance."

"Really, you make me almost want to laugh," said the puppet with a little toss of his head.

"Hey, Pinocchio," shouted the biggest of the boys, going right up to him. "Don't play the big shot around here; don't be such a show-off! Because if you're not afraid of us, we're not afraid of you, either. Remember that you're alone, and there are seven of us."

"Seven, like the seven deadly sins," said Pinocchio with a hearty laugh.

"Did you hear that? He insulted all of us! He called us the seven deadly sins!"

"Pinocchio, apologize to us for that insult, or else it'll be too bad for you!"

"Cuckoo!" went the puppet, tapping the tip of his nose with his forefinger, as a sign he was mocking them.

"Pinocchio, there's going to be trouble!"

"Cuckoo!"

"You'll get the beating of a jackass!"

"Cuckoo!"

"You'll go home with a broken nose!"

"Cuckoo!"

"I'll give you a cuckoo!" yelled the boldest of the urchins. "Take this to start with, and keep it for your supper tonight."

And as he said this, he pasted a blow on the puppet's head.

But it was tit for tat, as the saying goes, because the puppet, as was to be expected, answered right away with another blow; and in no time at all the battle became general and furious.

Although he was alone, Pinocchio defended himself heroically. With those hard wooden feet he managed so well that he kept his foes at a respectful distance. Wherever his feet could reach and strike, they left a bruise as a reminder.

Then the boys, vexed at not being able to fight close up with the puppet, decided to take up missiles; and undoing their bundles of books, they began to hurl their primers, their grammars, their storybooks, and other schoolbooks. But the puppet, who had quick and sharp eyes, always ducked in time, so that all the books sailed over his head and landed in the sea.

Just imagine the fish! Thinking that those books were something good to eat, the fish hurried in shoals to the surface of the water; but after nibbling at a few pages or at a frontispiece, they spat them out, making the sort of face that seemed to say: "That's not for us; we're used to feeding on much better fare."

Meanwhile, the battle was getting fiercer all the time, when suddenly a big Crab, who had come out of the water and climbed very slowly right onto the beach, blared out in a harsh voice like a trombone with a cold:

"Stop it, you good-for-nothing rascals! These fist-fights between boys seldom come to any good. Something bad always happens."

Poor Crab! It was just as if he had preached to the wind. In fact, that scamp of a Pinocchio, turning around with a fierce look, spoke rudely to him:

"Shut up, tedious Crab! You'd do better to suck on a couple of lichen drops to cure that hoarse throat of yours. Why don't you go to bed and try to sweat it off!"

In the meantime, the boys, who had now finished throwing all their own books, caught sight of the puppet's bundle of books nearby, and in no time at all they got hold of it.

Among the books there was a volume bound in thick cardboard, with its spine and corners in parchment. It was a manual of arithmetic. I leave it to you to imagine how heavy it was!

One of those urchins grabbed the volume and, taking aim at Pinocchio's head, let it fly with all his might. But instead of hitting the puppet, it struck the head of one of his own comrades, who turned as white as a sheet and could only say:

"Oh mother, help me...I'm dying!"

Then he fell full-length on the sand.

At the sight of that poor little inert figure, the frightened boys took to their heels in a hurry; and in a few moments they were out of sight.

But Pinocchio stayed behind; and although he was more dead than alive from grief and fright, he nonetheless ran to soak his handkerchief in the sea and began to bathe his poor schoolmate's temples. All the while, crying uncontrollably and wailing, he called him by name and said:

"Eugene! Poor Eugene! Open your eyes and look at me! Why don't you answer? It wasn't me who hurt you like that, really! Believe me, it wasn't me! Open your eyes, Eugene! If you keep your eyes closed, you'll make me die too. Oh, my God, how can I go back home now? How can I dare face my good mother? What will become of me? Where can I run away to? Where can I go to hide? Oh, how much better, a thousand times better, it would have been if I had gone to school! Why did I listen to my comrades, who are my ruination? And the teacher had warned me! And my mother had repeated it to me: 'Beware of bad company!' But I'm a stubborn and pig-headed fool. I let them all talk, and then I do as I please! And afterward I have to pay for it. That's why ever since I was born I've never had fifteen minutes of peace. My God, what's to become of me, what's to become of me, what's to become of me?"

And Pinocchio continued to cry, howl, beat at his head, and call poor Eugene by name when all of a sudden he heard a muffled sound of approaching footsteps.

He turned around; and there were two carabinieri.

"What are you doing stretched out on the ground there?" they asked Pinocchio.

"I'm helping this schoolmate of mine."

"Has he been taken ill?"

"I think so...."

"I'll say he's ill!" said one of the carabinieri, stooping down and looking closely at Eugene. "This boy has been wounded in the temple. Who was it that struck him?"

"Not me," stammered the puppet, who was breathless.

"If it wasn't you, then who was it that struck him?"

"Not me," repeated Pinocchio.

"What was he struck with?"

"With this book." And the puppet picked up the manual of arithmetic, bound in cardboard and parchment, to show it to the carabiniere.

"And whose book is this?"

"Mine."

"Enough. That's all we need to know. Get up right away and come along with us."

"But I—"

"Come along with us!"

"But I'm innocent—"

"Come along with us!"

Before setting off, the carabinieri called out to some fishermen who just then happened to be going by in their boat close to shore, and said to them:

"We're leaving this boy who's been wounded in the head in your care. Take him home with you and look after him. We'll be back tomorrow to see him."

Then they turned to Pinocchio and, having placed him between them, in a curt, military tone they commanded:

"March! and move fast! if not, so much the worse for you!"

Without waiting to have it repeated, the puppet began moving down the path that led to town. But the poor devil no longer knew what in the world was going on. He thought he was dreaming; and what a horrible dream! He was beside himself. His eyes saw everything double, his legs were shaking, his tongue stuck to the roof of his mouth, and he couldn't utter a single word. And yet, in the midst of that stupor and bewilderment of his, there was one sharp thorn that pierced his heart: the thought, that is, of having to pass beneath the window of his good Fairy's house, walking between two carabinieri. He would rather have died.

They had already reached the town and were about to enter when a strong gust of wind blew Pinocchio's cap off, carrying it some ten yards or so away.

"Is it all right if I go and retrieve my cap?" the puppet asked the carabinieri.

"Go ahead, but let's make it quick."

The puppet went and picked up his cap, but instead of putting it on his head, he put it in his mouth, between his teeth, and began to run as fast as he could toward the seashore. He sped like a rifle shot.

Deciding that it would be hard for them to catch up with him, the carabinieri set a huge mastiff after him, one that had won first prize in all the dog races. Pinocchio ran, but the dog ran even faster, so that all the people looked out the windows and flocked into the middle of the street, eager to see the conclusion of that fierce chase. But they were unable to satisfy their curiosity, because, between them, the mastiff and Pinocchio raised such a cloud of dust along the street that in a few moments it wasn't possible to see anything more.

CHAPTER XXVIII

Pinocchio runs the risk of being fried in a pan like a fish.

uring that frantic chase, there was a terrible moment when Pinocchio felt he was lost, because, you see, Alidoro—that was the mastiff's name—kept on running and running until he had almost caught up with him.

Suffice it to say that the puppet heard the heavy panting of that awful beast a hand's breadth away and that he even felt the hot puffs of his breathing.

Fortunately, the shore was now nearby and the sea was in sight only a few steps away.

As soon as he got to the shore, the puppet took a splendid leap, just as a frog might have done, and landed in the middle of the water. Alidoro tried to stop, but carried forward by the impetus of the chase, he went into the water too. Now, the poor wretch didn't know how to swim, so right away he began thrashing with his paws, trying to keep afloat. But the more he struggled, the more his head went under.

When he managed to get his head above water again, the poor dog's eyes were wild with terror, and he barked out:

"I'm drowning! I'm drowning!"

"Croak!" Pinocchio answered from afar, seeing himself safe from all danger now.

"Help me, dear Pinocchio! Save me from death!"

At those anguished cries, the puppet, who really had a very good heart, was moved to pity; and turning to the dog, he said:

"But if I do save you, will you promise not to bother me anymore and not to chase me?"

"I promise! I promise! Hurry, for mercy's sake, because if you wait even another half minute I'll be dead and gone!"

Pinocchio hesitated a little; but then, recalling that his father had often told him that a good deed never goes for naught, he swam hard to reach Alidoro, and taking hold of him by the tail with both hands he brought him safe and sound onto the dry sand of the beach.

The poor dog couldn't even stand up. In spite of himself, he had drunk so much saltwater that he was swollen like a balloon. Even so, the puppet, not daring to be too trustful, thought it wiser to jump back into the sea; and as he struck out from shore, he called back to the friend he had rescued:

"Farewell, Alidoro; bon voyage, and best wishes to the folks at home."

"Farewell, Pinocchio," answered the dog; "a thousand thanks for having saved me from death. You've done me a great service, and in this world one good turn deserves another. If the chance ever arises, I won't forget it."

Pinocchio went on swimming, always keeping close to land. At last he felt he had reached a safe place, and giving a look toward the shore he saw a sort of cave among the rocks, with a long column of smoke rising from it.

"In that cave," he said to himself then, "there must be a fire. That's all to the good. I'll go dry myself and warm up, and then...and then let happen what may."

Having made up his mind, he swam toward the rocks; but just as he was about to scramble up them he felt something under the water that kept rising, rising, rising and that lifted him up right into the air. He tried to escape, but it was too late now, because to his great astonishment he found himself trapped in a large net, amid a swarming mass of fish of all shapes and sizes that were wriggling and writhing like so many souls in torment.

At the same time, he saw such an ugly fisherman come out of the cave, really so ugly that he looked like a monster from the deep. Instead of hair, he had a very thick clump of green weeds on his head; green was the skin of his body; green his eyes; and green his long beard that reached all the way down to the ground. He looked like a huge green lizard standing upright on its hind legs.

When the fisherman had drawn in the net from the sea, he exclaimed with joy:

"The Lord be praised! Today, too, I'll be able to have a bellyful of fish!"

"It's a good thing I'm not a fish!" said Pinocchio to himself, cheering up.

The net full of fish was brought into the cave; a dark smoke-blackened cave in the middle of which was a large frying pan with sizzling oil that sent up a delicious smell such as to cut your breath short.

"Now, let's see what kind of fish we've caught," said the green fisherman; and sticking his hand, which was so huge that it looked like a baker's peel, into the net, he pulled out a handful of red mullet.

"Very nice, these red mullet!" he said, looking at them and sniffing them with satisfaction. And after sniffing them, he flung them into a large earthen pot without any water in it.

Then he repeated the same operation several times; and as he drew out the other fish, his mouth watered and he gloated:

"Very nice, these hake!"

"Exquisite, these gray mullet!"

"Delicious, these sole!"

"Choice, these sea bass!"

"Pretty, these anchovies with their heads on!"

As you can imagine, the hake, the gray mullet, the sole, the bass, and the anchovies all went together pell-mell into the earthen pot to keep the red mullet company.

The last to remain in the net was Pinocchio.

As soon as the fisherman had pulled him out, he opened his enormous green eyes wide in amazement and cried out half-frightened:

"What sort of fish is this? I don't recall ever having eaten fish of this shape or form!"

He looked at him again, carefully; and after looking him all over closely, he finally said:

"I know; it must be a sea crab."

Then Pinocchio, mortified at hearing himself taken for a crab, said crossly:

"What do you mean, a crab? Be careful how you treat me! For your information, I'm a puppet."

"A puppet?" replied the fisherman. "To tell the truth, a puppet-fish is a new fish to me. So much the better; I'll eat you with all the more relish."

"Eat me? But won't you understand that I'm not a fish? Can't you hear that I talk and reason the way you do?"

"That's quite true," the fisherman continued, "and since I see that you're a fish that has the good fortune to talk and reason like me, I intend to treat you with all due respect."

"And what does this respect consist of?"

"As a token of my friendship and high esteem, I'll let you choose the way you want to be cooked. Do you want to be fried in a skillet, or do you prefer to be cooked in a pan with tomato sauce?"

"To tell the truth," replied Pinocchio, "if I'm to choose, I prefer rather to be set free, so I can go back home."

"You're joking! Do you think I want to lose the chance of tasting so rare a fish? It isn't every day that a puppet-fish comes along in these waters. I know what I'll do; I'll fry you in a skillet with the other fish, and you'll be glad of it. There's always some comfort in being fried in company with others."

At this tune, the wretched Pinocchio began to cry, to scream, to plead; and as he wept, he said:

"How much better it would have been if I had gone to school! I preferred to listen to my comrades, and now I'm paying for it. Boo-hoo-hoo!"

And because he squirmed like an eel and made such frantic efforts to slip out of the clutches of the green fisherman, the latter took a nice length of reed, and after tying the puppet's hands and feet like a salami, he threw him into the bottom of the pot with the others.

Then, getting a large old wooden platter that was full of flour, he busied himself with rolling all those fish in it; and as he covered them with flour, he threw them one by one to be fried in the skillet.

The first to dance in the boiling oil were the poor hake; then it fell to the bass, then to the gray mullet, then to the sole and the anchovies; and finally it was Pinocchio's turn. Seeing himself so near death (and what a terrible death!) he was seized by such trembling and by such terror that he could no longer find voice or breath to beg for mercy.

The poor boy pleaded with his eyes! But without even paying any attention to him, the green fisherman rolled him in the flour five or six times, covering him so well from head to foot that he seemed to have turned into a plaster puppet.

Then he took him by the head, and....

Pinocchio returns to the Fairy's house, and she promises him that the next day he will no longer be a puppet but will become a boy. A grand breakfast is planned to celebrate this great event.

ust as the fisherman was about to throw Pinocchio into the skillet, a huge dog came into the cave, drawn there by the pungent, enticing smell of the frying fish.

"Go away," hollered the fisherman, threatening him and still holding the flour-coated puppet in his hand.

But the poor dog was absolutely famished; and yelping and wagging his tail, he seemed to say:

"Give me a bit of fried fish and I'll leave you alone."

"Go away, I said!" repeated the fisherman; and he raised his leg to give him a kick.

Then the dog, who didn't take any sass when he was really hungry, turned and snarled at the fisherman, baring his horrible fangs.

Just then a small voice, ever so faint, was heard in the cave saying:

"Save me, Alidoro! If you don't save me, I'm done!"

The dog recognized Pinocchio's voice at once, and to his great astonishment he noticed that the faint voice had come from the flour-coated bundle that the fisherman was holding in his hand.

And what does he do then? He takes a great leap from the ground, snaps up the flour-coated bundle in his mouth, and holding it gingerly between his teeth, runs out of the cave and is off like a flash.

Enraged at seeing a fish he was so anxious to eat snatched from his hand, the fisherman started to run after the dog; but after going a few steps he was seized with a fit of coughing and had to go back.

Meanwhile, when Alidoro got to the path leading to the town, he stopped and gently put his friend Pinocchio down on the ground.

"How thankful I am to you!" said the puppet.

"There's no need to thank me," replied the dog. "You saved me first, and one good turn deserves another. It's a fact; in this world we must help one another."

"But how did you ever happen to come to that cave?"

"I was still lying there on the beach more dead than alive when the wind brought me the delicious smell of something frying at a distance. That delicious smell whetted my appetite, and I followed it. If I had arrived a minute later!"

"Don't say it!" shouted Pinocchio, who was still trembling with fear. "Don't say it! If you had arrived a minute later, by now I would have already been fried, eaten, and digested. Brrr! I get the shivers just thinking of it!"

Laughing, Alidoro stretched his right paw out to the puppet, who clasped it fervently as a token of deep friendship. And then they parted.

The dog went homeward; and Pinocchio, left alone, went to a hut nearby and spoke to an old man who was sunning himself in front of the door.

"Tell me, good sir, do you know anything about a poor boy named Eugene who was hurt in the head?"

"The boy was brought to this hut by some fishermen, and now—"

"He's probably dead now!" interjected Pinocchio, with great anguish.

"No, he's alive now and has already returned home."

"Really, really?" cried the puppet, jumping for joy. "Then the wound wasn't serious?"

"But it could have been quite serious, and even fatal," answered the old man, "because somebody threw a big, cardboard-bound book at his head."

"Who threw it at him?"

"A schoolmate of his, a certain Pinocchio."

"And who is this Pinocchio?" the puppet asked, playing dumb.

"They say that he's a young rowdy, a vagabond, a real madcap of a boy."

"Lies, all lies!"

"Do you know this Pinocchio?"

"By sight," answered the puppet.

"And what's your opinion of him?" the old man asked him.

"I think he's a splendid fellow, fond of school, obedient, and very attached to his father and his family...."

While he was reeling off all these lies with a straight face, the puppet happened to touch his nose and noticed that it had grown by a palm's length. Then, all in a fright he began to exclaim:

"Don't believe all the nice things I've told you about him, good sir; because I know Pinocchio very well, and I too can assure you that he really is a rowdy. He's disobedient and he's a loafer who instead of going to school goes around with his comrades to make trouble."

As soon as he had uttered these words, his nose shortened and returned to its natural length, as it was before.

"Why are you all white like that?" the old man asked him suddenly.

"Well, you see...without noticing it, I rubbed against a wall that had just been whitewashed," replied the puppet, ashamed to confess that he had been rolled in flour like a fish meant to be fried in a skillet.

"And what about your jacket, your trousers, and your cap? What have you done with them?"

"I ran into thieves, and they stripped me. Tell me, good old man, would you happen to have some old clothes to give me, just so I can go home?"

"As for clothes, my boy, all I have is a small sack in which I keep lupine seeds. Take it, if you like; it's right there."

Pinocchio didn't wait to be told a second time. He quickly took the lupine sack, which was empty, made a little hole at the bottom with scissors, and a hole on each side, and slipped it on like a shirt. And scantily dressed like that, he set off for town.

But along the way he didn't feel at all at ease, so that he would take one step forward and then one backward; and talking to himself, he kept repeating:

"How can I face my dear good Fairy? What will she say when she sees me? Will she forgive me for this second escapade? I bet she won't forgive me. Oh, she certainly won't forgive me! And it serves me right, because I'm a brat, always promising to reform and never keeping my word."

When he reached the town it was already late at night; and because it was horrid weather, with the rain coming down in bucketfuls, he went straight to the Fairy's house determined to knock at the door and make his way in.

But when he got there, he felt his courage fail, and instead of knocking he ran back away from it some twenty steps or so. Then he went up to the door a second time, but nothing came of it. Then he approached a third time, and again nothing. The fourth time, he took the iron knocker tremblingly in his hand and gave a faint little knock.

He waited and waited, until finally after half an hour a window opened on the top floor—the house had four floors—and Pinocchio saw a large Snail with a little lighted lamp on her head look out. She said:

"Who is it at this hour?"

"Is the Fairy at home?" the puppet asked.

"The Fairy is sleeping and does not want to be awakened. Who are you, anyway?"

"It's me."

"'Me' who?"

"Pinocchio."

"Pinocchio who?"

"The puppet; the one who lives with the Fairy."

"Ah, I see," said the Snail. "Wait for me there; I'll come down and open the door for you right away."

"Hurry, for pity's sake, because I'm freezing to death."

"My boy, I am a snail, and snails are never in a hurry."

Meanwhile an hour passed; and then two hours passed, but the door didn't open. So Pinocchio, who was shivering on account of the cold, the fear, and the drenching he was getting, plucked up his courage and knocked a second time; and he knocked harder.

At this second knock a window opened on the next floor down, and the same Snail looked out.

"Dear little Snail," called Pinocchio from the street, "I've been waiting for two hours! And two hours in such a wretched night as this seem longer than two years. Hurry, for pity's sake."

"My boy," answered that little creature from the window, quite calm and unperturbed, "my boy, I am a snail, and snails are never in a hurry."

And the window closed again.

A short while later midnight struck; then one o'clock, then two o'clock; but the door was still shut.

So Pinocchio, losing all patience, grasped the door knocker angrily, intending to give a bang that would deafen everyone in the building; but the knocker, which was made of iron, suddenly became a live eel that wriggled out of his hands and disappeared into the small stream of water going down the middle of the street.

"Oh, is that so?" shouted Pinocchio, blinder than ever with rage. "If the knocker has disappeared, I'll just go on knocking by kicking."

And backing up a little, he let go a whopping kick at the door, so hard that his foot went halfway through; and when the puppet tried to pull it back

out, it proved to be a hopeless effort because his foot was stuck tight there like a riveted nail.

Imagine poor Pinocchio! He had to spend the rest of the night with one foot on the ground, and the other up in the air.

In the morning, at dawn, the door finally opened. To come down from the fourth floor to the front door, that clever little creature, the Snail, had taken but nine hours. You really have to say that she had worked up quite a sweat.

"What are you doing with that foot of yours stuck in the door?" she asked, laughing at the puppet.

"It was an accident. Dear little Snail, try to see if you can free me from this torture."

"My boy, it takes a carpenter for that job, and I have never been a carpenter."

"Beg the Fairy for me!"

"The Fairy is sleeping and does not want to be awakened."

"But what do you expect me to do, nailed all day to this door?"

"Amuse yourself by counting the ants that go by."

"At least bring me something to eat, because I feel faint."

"Right away!" said the Snail.

In fact, after three and a half hours, Pinocchio saw her returning with a silver tray on her head. On the tray there was bread, a roast chicken, and four ripe apricots.

"Here is the breakfast sent to you by the Fairy," said the Snail.

At the sight of all those good things, the puppet's spirits were raised. But how great was his disappointment when, on beginning to eat, he was forced to acknowledge that the bread was of chalk, the chicken of cardboard, and the four apricots of alabaster, painted to look real.

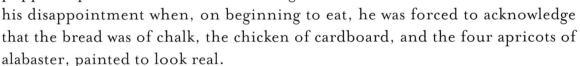

He wanted to cry, to give up in despair, to throw away the tray and everything on it; but instead, either because of his grief or because of the empty feeling in his stomach, the fact is that he fainted.

When he came to, he found himself stretched out on a sofa, with the Fairy by his side.

"I will forgive you this time too," the Fairy said to him, "but it will be too bad for you if you play me another of your pranks."

Pinocchio promised and swore that he would study and that he would always behave himself. And he kept his word throughout the rest of the school year. Indeed, at the exams before vacation time he had the honor of being the best student in school; and his general conduct was considered so satisfactory and so praiseworthy that the Fairy said to him:

"Tomorrow at last your wish will be granted."

"That is?"

"Tomorrow you are to stop being a wooden puppet, and you will become a proper boy."

Anyone who didn't see Pinocchio's joy at this longed-for news can never imagine what it was like. All his friends and schoolmates were to be invited the next day to a grand breakfast in the Fairy's house to celebrate together the great event; and the Fairy made preparations for two hundred cups of caffè-e-latte and four hundred buns buttered on the inside and on the outside. It promised to be a great and joyous day, but....

Unfortunately, in the lives of puppets, there is always a "but" that spoils everything.

CHAPTER XXX

Instead of becoming a boy, Pinocchio goes off secretly with his friend Candlewick to Funland.

s is only natural, Pinocchio immediately asked the Fairy for permission to go around the town to extend the invitations, and the Fairy said:

"Go right ahead and invite your comrades to tomorrow's breakfast, but remember to return home before it gets dark. Do you understand?"

"I promise to be back in an hour," replied the puppet.

"Take care, Pinocchio! Children are quick to make promises, but most of the time they are slow in keeping them."

"But I'm not like the others; when I say something, I mean it."

"We shall see. If you should disobey, though, it will be much the worse for you."

"Why?"

"Because children who don't heed the advice of those who know better than they do always end up in some kind of trouble."

"And I know that from experience!" exclaimed Pinocchio. "But I won't fall into the same trap again."

"We shall see if you are telling the truth."

Without adding another word, the puppet said good-bye to his good Fairy, who was like a mother to him, and went out the front door, singing and dancing.

In just about an hour all his friends had been invited. Some of them accepted at once and eagerly; others waited to be coaxed at first, but when they learned that the buns to be dunked in the caffè-e-latte would even be buttered on the outside, they all ended by saying: "We'll come too, as a favor to you."

Now you should know that among his schoolmates, Pinocchio had one who was his favorite, who was very dear to him, and whose name was Romeo; but everybody called him by his nickname Candlewick because of his scrawny little frame, just like the new wick of a night-lamp.

Candlewick was the laziest and the most roguish boy in the whole school, but Pinocchio was extremely fond of him. In fact, he went right away to look for him at his house so as to invite him to the breakfast, but he didn't find him.

He went back a second time, but Candlewick wasn't there. He went back a third time, but to no avail.

Where could he dig him up? He looked high and low for him, and finally saw him hiding under the portico of a peasant's house.

"What are you doing there?" asked Pinocchio, going up to him.

"I'm waiting for midnight, so I can run away."

"Where are you going?"

"Far, far, far away!"

"I went to your house three times to look for you!"

"What did you want me for?"

"Don't you know about the great event? Don't you know about my good luck?"

"What is it?"

"Tomorrow I stop being a puppet and I become a boy like you and all the others."

"A lot of good may it do you."

"So I expect you for breakfast tomorrow, at my house."

"But I've just told you that I'm leaving tonight."

"At what time?"

"In a little while."

"But where are you going?"

"I'm going to live in a land that's the most beautiful land in the world: really easy living and merriment."

"What is it called?"

"It's called Funland. Why don't you come too?"

"Me? Certainly not!"

"You're making a mistake, Pinocchio! Believe me, if you don't come you'll regret it. Where do you expect to find a more wholesome place for us kids? There are no schools there; there are no teachers there; there are no books there. They never study in that blessed land. There's no school on Thursday, and every week is made up of six Thursdays and a Sunday. Just think that vacation begins on the first of January and ends on the last day of December. Now that's the sort of place that appeals to me! That's how all civilized countries should be!"

"But how do they pass the days there in Funland?"

"The days go by in play and good times from morning till night. Then at night you go to bed, and the next morning you begin all over again. What do you think of that?"

"Hmm!" went Pinocchio, and he nodded his head slightly, as though to say: "It's a life that I too would gladly lead!"

"So then, do you want to leave with me? Yes or no? Make up your mind."

"No, no, a thousand times no. I've promised my good Fairy to become a good boy now, and I intend to keep my word. In fact, now that I see the sun is going down, I have to leave you and run. Good-bye, then; and bon voyage."

"Where are you rushing off to?"

"Home. My good Fairy wants me to be back before dark."

"Wait another two minutes."

"Then I'll be too late."

"Just two minutes."

"And what if the Fairy yells at me?"

"Let her yell. When she's tired of yelling, she'll calm down," said that scapegrace of a Candlewick.

"But how will you manage? Are you going alone or with others?"

"Alone? There'll be more than a hundred of us kids."

"And are you making the trip by foot?"

"In a little while the wagon's coming by to pick me up and take me all the way, within the boundaries of that happy land."

"I'd give anything to have the wagon pass by now!"

"Why?"

"To see all of you going off together."

"Wait here a little longer and you will see us."

"No, no; I want to go back home."

"Wait another two minutes."

"I've already waited too long. The Fairy must be worrying about me."

"Poor Fairy! Is she afraid that the bats will eat you?"

"But then," continued Pinocchio, "you're really sure that there are absolutely no schools in that land?"

"Not even the ghost of one."

"And not even schoolteachers?"

"Not a single one."

"And nobody ever has to study?"

"Never, never, never!"

"What a wonderful land!" said Pinocchio, his mouth watering. "What a wonderful land! I've never been there, but I can just imagine it."

"Why don't you come too?"

"It's no use for you to tempt me! I've promised my good Fairy to be a sensible boy now, and I don't want to go back on my word."

"Well, farewell then, and give my best regards to the grammar schools…and the high schools too, if you meet them on the way."

"Farewell, Candlewick; have a good journey, have fun and remember your friends sometimes."

Having said this, the puppet took a few steps as if to leave; but then, stopping and turning to his friend, he asked him:

"But are you really sure that in that land all the weeks are made up of six Thursdays and a Sunday?"

"Quite sure!"

"But are you positive that vacation time begins on the first of January and ends on the last day of December?"

"Quite positive!"

"What a wonderful land!" repeated Pinocchio, spitting out of sheer delight. Then, taking a resolute stance, he quickly added:

"Well, good-bye for real, and bon voyage."

"Good-bye."

"How soon will you be leaving?"

"In a little while!"

"That's too bad! If it were only an hour before you leave, I might almost wait."

"And the Fairy?"

"I'm already late anyway, and to go home an hour sooner or an hour later doesn't matter."

"Poor Pinocchio! And what if the Fairy yells at you?"

"So what! I'll let her yell. When she's tired of yelling, she'll calm down."

Meanwhile night had fallen and it was quite dark, when all of a sudden they saw a dim light moving in the distance; and they heard a sound of harness bells and the blare of a trumpet, but so faint and muffled that it seemed like the buzzing of a mosquito.

"There it is!" shouted Candlewick, getting to his feet.

"Who is it?" asked Pinocchio in a low voice.

"It's the wagon that's coming to pick me up. Well, are you coming, yes or no?"

"But is it really true," the puppet asked, "that in that land kids never have to study?"

"Never, never, never!"

"What a wonderful land, what a wonderful land, what a wonderful land!"

After five months of fun and easy living, Pinocchio wakes to a disagreeable surprise.

A t last the wagon arrived; and it arrived without making the slightest noise, because its wheels were swathed in rags and tow.

It was drawn by twelve pairs of donkeys, all of the same size, but with different colored coats.

Some were ashen gray, some white, others were speckled in the manner of pepper and salt, and others had wide stripes of yellow and blue.

But the most curious thing of all was this: those twelve pairs, that is, those twenty-four donkeys, instead of being shod like all other draft animals or beasts of burden, had men's boots of white leather on their feet.

And the driver of the wagon?

Picture a little man more wide than tall, soft and oily like a lump of butter, with a small face like a rosy apple, a little mouth that was always smiling, and a thin wheedling voice like that of a cat appealing to the tender heart of the mistress of the house.

All boys were charmed by him as soon as they saw him and fought with one another in getting up into his wagon so as to be taken by him to that true land of heart's desire known on the geographical map by the seductive name of Funland.

In fact the wagon was already full of young boys between eight and twelve years old, piled one on top of the other like anchovies in brine. They were uncomfortable, they were squeezed together, and they could hardly breathe; but nobody said "Ow!" and nobody complained. The consolation of knowing that in a few hours they would reach a land where there were no books, no schools, and no teachers made them so pleased and so patient that they didn't feel any discomfort, or hardship, or hunger, or thirst, or sleepiness.

As soon as the wagon had stopped, the little man turned to Candlewick, and with a thousand mincing ways and words he asked him, smiling:

"Tell me, my handsome lad, do you want to come to that happy land too?"

"You bet I want to come."

"But I warn you, my dear, there's no more room in the wagon. As you see, it's quite full."

"That's all right!" replied Candlewick, "if there's no room inside, I'll put up with sitting on the shafts of the wagon."

And with a jump he mounted astride the shafts.

"And you, my love," said the little man, turning ceremoniously to Pinocchio, "what do you intend to do? Are you coming with us or staying?"

"I'm staying," answered Pinocchio. "I want to go back home. I want to study and do well at school, the way all good boys do."

"A lot of good may it do you!"

"Pinocchio!" said Candlewick then. "Listen to me; come away with us, and we'll have a wonderful time."

"No, no, no!"

"Come away with us, and we'll have a wonderful time," shouted four other voices from within the wagon.

"Come away with us, and we'll have a wonderful time," yelled a hundred or so voices all together from within the wagon.

"But if I come with you, what will my good Fairy say?" said the puppet, who was beginning to soften and waver.

"Don't wrap your head in such gloomy thoughts. Just think that we're going to a place where we'll be free to make a hullabaloo from morning to night."

Pinocchio didn't answer, but he heaved a sigh. Then he heaved another sigh; and then a third sigh. Finally, he said:

"Make some room for me. I want to come too."

"The places are all taken," replied the little man, "but to show you how welcome you are, I can give you my place on the box."

"And you?"

"And I'll go along on foot."

"No, really; I won't let you do that. I'd rather get up on the back of one of these donkeys," cried Pinocchio.

So saying, he went up to the right-hand donkey of the first pair and made as if to mount him. But the creature, swerving around unexpectedly, butted him hard in the stomach and sent him sprawling with his legs in the air.

Just imagine the hoots and howls of laughter of all those boys who were looking on.

But the little man didn't laugh. He went up ever so lovingly to the rebellious donkey, and while making as though to give him a kiss bit off half of his right ear.

Meanwhile, Pinocchio got up from the ground in a rage and with one leap sprang onto the poor animal's back. And it was such a magnificent leap that the boys stopped their laughter and began to shout: "Hurrah for Pinocchio!" clapping wildly as if they would never stop.

But all of a sudden the donkey kicked up both his hind legs, bucking so violently that he threw the poor puppet onto a heap of gravel in the middle of the road.

At that, there were renewed howls of laughter. But the little man, instead of laughing, was overcome by so much tenderness for that cute, fretful donkey, that with a kiss he took half of his other ear clean off. Then he said to the puppet:

"Get back up on him, and don't be afraid. That donkey had some whim or other in his head; but I've whispered a few sweet words in his ear, and I think I've got him to be gentle and sensible."

Pinocchio got on, and the wagon started off. But while the donkeys were galloping along and the wagon was rolling over the cobblestones of the highway, the puppet thought he heard a low, barely audible voice that said to him:

"Poor simpleton; you wanted your own way, but you'll regret it."

Somewhat frightened, Pinocchio looked all around to find out where the words came from, but he didn't see any-one: the donkeys were galloping, the wagon was rolling along, the boys inside the wagon were sleeping, Candlewick was snoring like a dormouse, and the little man, sitting on the driver's box, was singing to himself in a low voice between his teeth:

Everybody sleeps at night,
But never asleep am I....

After another half mile, Pinocchio heard the same faint voice say to him:

"Remember this, you silly fool! Boys who give up studying and turn their backs on books, schools, and teachers to do nothing but play games and have fun are bound to come to a bad end. I know from experience, and so I can tell you. A day will come when you'll cry too, just as I'm crying now; but it will be too late then."

At these words, which were whispered in a low tone, the puppet, more frightened than ever, jumped down from his mount and went to take hold of the donkey by the muzzle.

But imagine his surprise when he found that the donkey was crying—and crying just like a boy!

"Hey, Mister little man," shouted Pinocchio to the wagon owner, "do you know what? This donkey is crying."

"Let him cry; he'll laugh on his wedding day."

"Did you by any chance teach him how to talk?"

"No; he learned how to mumble a few words on his own during the three years he lived with a company of performing dogs."

"Poor beast!"

"Come, come," said the little man, "let's not waste time watching a donkey cry. Get back on, and let's get going. It's a cold night, and it's a long way."

Pinocchio obeyed without breathing another word. The wagon rolled on again, and the next morning at daybreak they arrived safely in Funland.

This land didn't resemble any other place in the world. Its population was made up entirely of boys. The oldest were fourteen, the youngest barely eight years old. In the streets there was such gaiety, such a din, such wild shouting as to take your head off! Groups of urchins were everywhere. Some were playing at walnuts, some at quoits, some at ball. Some were riding bicycles, some were on wooden horses. Here a group played blindman's buff; there a group played tag; others, dressed as clowns, played at swallowing burning tow; some were acting, some were singing, some were turning somersaults, some were having fun walking on their hands with their feet in the air; some rolled hoops, some strutted about dressed as generals with paper helmets and cardboard sabres; some laughed, some yelled, some called to others, some clapped their hands, some whistled, some imitated hens cackling after laying eggs. In short, such pandemonium, such screeching, such a wild tumult, that you needed cotton wool in your ears to keep from going deaf. In every square you could see canvas puppet theaters crowded with boys from morning till night; and on all the walls of the houses you could read, written in charcoal, such choice sayings as these: "Hurray for phun and gams!" (instead of "fun and games"), "We don't want no more skools!" (instead of "We don't want any more schools"), "Down with Uhrit Matik!" (instead of "arithmetic"), and other such gems.

Pinocchio, Candlewick, and all the other boys who had made the trip with the little man had no sooner set foot in this town than they plunged into the midst of the hullabaloo, and in a few minutes, as you can readily imagine, they became friends with everyone. Could anyone be happier, could anyone be more satisfied than they?

In the midst of continual amusements and games of all sorts, the hours, the days, the weeks passed like lightning.

"Oh, what a beautiful life!" Pinocchio would say, whenever he happened to run into Candlewick.

"Do you see now that I was right?" the latter would retort. "And to think that you didn't want to leave! To think that you had taken it into your head to go back home to your Fairy and waste your time studying! If you've escaped from the nuisance of books and schools now, you owe it to me, to my advice and concern. Don't you agree? It's only true friends who can do such big favors."

"That's true, Candlewick. If I'm really a happy boy today, the credit is all yours. And yet, do you know what our teacher used to say: 'Don't go around with that rogue of a Candlewick, because Candlewick is bad company and his advice can only lead you astray.'"

"Poor teacher!" replied the other, shaking his head. "I know only too well that he couldn't stand me and that he always enjoyed maligning me; but I'm noble-minded and so I forgive him!"

"Magnanimous soul!" said Pinocchio, embracing his friend warmly and kissing him between the eyes.

And so five months had already gone by in this wonderful life of ease passed in fun and games all day long without ever coming face to face with a book or a school, when Pinocchio, on waking up one morning, had, as we are wont to say, a rather disagreeable surprise that really put him in a bad mood.

Pinocchio gets donkey ears, and then turns into a real donkey and begins to bray.

nd what was the surprise?

I'll tell you, my dear little readers: the surprise was that Pinocchio, on waking up, quite naturally happened to scratch his head; and in scratching his head he noticed....

Can you possibly guess what he noticed?

To his great amazement, he noticed that his ears had grown more than a palm's width.

You remember that ever since his birth the puppet had tiny, tiny ears, so tiny that they couldn't even be seen with the naked eye. Now just imagine how he felt when he realized that during the night his ears had grown so long that they looked like two dusters made of sedge.

Right away he looked for a mirror so he could see himself; but not finding a mirror, he filled the washstand basin with water, and reflecting himself in it, saw what he would never have wanted to see: that is, he saw his image adorned with a magnificent pair of asinine ears.

I leave you to think of poor Pinocchio's anguish, shame, and despair.

He began to cry, to scream, to beat his head against the wall; but the more he carried on, the more his ears grew and grew and grew, becoming hairy toward the top.

At the sound of those piercing shrieks a pretty little Marmot, who lived on the floor above, came into the room; and seeing the puppet in such a frenzy, she asked him anxiously:

"What's wrong, my dear fellow-lodger?"

"I'm sick, dear Marmot, very sick...and sick with a disease that scares me. Do you know how to take a pulse?"

"A little."

"Feel mine then and see if by chance I have a fever."

The Marmot raised her right forepaw, and after having felt Pinocchio's pulse, said to him with a sigh:

"My friend, I'm sorry to have to give you some bad news."

"What is it?"

"You've got a terrible fever."

"But what kind of fever is it?"

"It's jackass fever."

"I don't understand what that sort of fever is," answered the puppet, who, alas, understood it only too well.

"Then I'll explain it to you," the Marmot went on. "I must tell you that in two or three hours you'll be neither a puppet nor a boy anymore."

"What'll I be then?"

"In two or three hours you'll become an actual donkey, just like the ones that pull carts and carry cabbage and lettuce to the market."

"Oh poor me! Poor me!" cried Pinocchio, seizing both his ears with his hands, and pulling and mauling them furiously as though they were somebody else's ears.

"My dear boy," continued the Marmot, to comfort him, "what can you do about it? That's the way it is. It's written in the Decrees of Wisdom that all lazy boys who hate books, schools, and teachers, and who spend their days in play and games and amusements, must end up sooner or later by turning into little jackasses."

"But is that really true?" asked the puppet, sobbing.

"Alas, that's the way it is. And crying doesn't do any good now. You should have thought of it before!"

"But it's not my fault; believe me, dear Marmot, it's all Candlewick's fault."

"And who is this Candlewick?"

"A schoolmate of mine. I wanted to go back home; I wanted to be obedient; I wanted to continue studying and do well...but Candlewick said to me: 'Why do you want to be bothered studying? Why do you want to go to school? Come with me to Funland instead; we'll never study there, we'll have fun from morning to night and always have a wonderful time.'"

"And why did you follow the advice of a false friend, such a bad companion?"

"Why?...because, dear Marmot, I'm a puppet without any sense...and without a heart. Oh, if I had had even the tiniest bit of heart I would never have deserted that good Fairy who loved me like a mother and who had done so much for me! By this time I wouldn't be a puppet anymore, but instead I'd be a fine boy like so many others. Oh...but if I meet Candlewick, it'll be too bad for him! I'll give him a piece of my mind!"

Then he made as if to go out, but when he reached the door he remembered that he had donkey's ears, and being ashamed to show them in public, what did he think of? He took a large cotton cap, stuck it on his head, and pulled it all the way down over the tip of his nose.

Then he went out and started looking everywhere for Candlewick. He looked for him in the streets, in the squares, in the little puppet shows, every place; but he didn't find him. He asked everyone he met along the way about him, but no one had seen him.

So then he went to look for him at his home, and when he got to the door he knocked.

"Who is it?" asked Candlewick from within.

"It's me," answered the puppet.

"Wait a moment, and I'll open for you."

After half an hour the door opened; and just imagine how surprised Pinocchio was when, on going into the room, he saw his friend Candlewick with a large cotton cap on his head that came down over his nose.

At the sight of that cap, Pinocchio almost felt relieved, and at once he thought to himself: "Can my friend be suffering from the same illness that I have? I wonder if he has jackass fever too?"

But pretending not to notice anything, he smiled and asked:

"How are you, my dear Candlewick?"

"Fine! Like a mouse in a wheel of Parmesan cheese."

"Do you really mean it?"

"Why should I lie to you?"

"Excuse me, my friend; but then why do you have that cotton cap on your head, covering your ears?"

"The doctor ordered it because I hurt myself in the knee. And you, dear Pinocchio, why are you wearing that cotton cap pulled all the way down over your nose?"

"The doctor ordered it because I scraped my foot."

"Oh, poor Pinocchio!"

"Oh, poor Candlewick!"

Following these words there was a long, long silence during which the two friends just looked at each other mockingly.

At last the puppet, in a honey-sweet, flutelike tone, said to his comrade:

"Just out of curiosity, my dear Candlewick, have you ever had anything wrong with your ears?"

"Never! How about you?"

"Never! Except that since this morning one of my ears has been killing me."

"I have the same trouble."

"You too? Which ear is it that hurts you?"

"Both of them. And you?"

"Both of them. Could it be the same illness?"

"I'm afraid so."

"Will you do me a favor, Candlewick?"

"Gladly! With all my heart!"

"Will you let me see your ears?"

"Why not? But first I want to see yours, dear Pinocchio."

"No, you have to be first."

"No, my dear fellow! You first, and then me."

"Well," the puppet said then, "let's make a gentleman's agreement."

"Let's hear the agreement."

"Let's take off our caps at the same time; do you agree?"

"I agree."

"All right, then, ready!" And Pinocchio began to count out loud: "One! Two! Three!"

At the word "three" the two boys took their caps off and threw them into the air.

And then a scene took place that would seem unbelievable if it weren't true. What happened was that when they saw they were both afflicted with the same misfortune, Pinocchio and Candlewick, instead of feeling ashamed and distressed, began to poke fun at each other's preposterously overgrown ears; and after a thousand coarse antics they ended by breaking into a good long laugh.

And they laughed and laughed and laughed so that they had to hold their sides; but at the height of their laughter Candlewick suddenly became silent, then, reeling about and changing color, he said to his friend:

"Help, Pinocchio, help!"

"What's wrong with you?"

"Oh, dear me! I can't stand up straight anymore."

"I can't either," exclaimed Pinocchio, crying and staggering.

And while they were talking like this, the two of them bent over on all fours and began running around the room on their hands and feet. And while they were running, their arms turned into legs with hoofs, their faces grew longer and turned into muzzles, and their backs became covered with a light-gray coat speckled with black.

But do you know what was the worst moment for those two wretches? The worst and most humiliating moment was when they felt a tail growing behind. Overcome with shame and grief then, they tried to cry and complain about their fate.

Would that they had never done so! Instead of moans and lamentations, they let out asinine brays; and braying loud and long, the two of them went in chorus:

"Hee-haw! Hee-haw! Hee-haw!"

Just then there was a knocking at the door, and a voice from outside said:

"Open up! It's me, the little man, the driver of the wagon that brought you to this place. Open at once, or it'll be too bad for you!"

Having become a real donkey, Pinocchio is bought by a circus Manager who wants to teach him how to dance and jump through hoops. But one evening he goes lame, and then he is bought by someone who wants to use his hide to make a drum.

eeing that the door didn't open, the little man burst it open with a violent kick; and when he had entered the room, he spoke to Pinocchio and Candlewick with his usual snigger:

"Well done, boys! You brayed beautifully, and I recognized you by your voices right away. And so, here I am."

At these words the two donkeys became silent and crestfallen, with their heads lowered, their ears turned down and their tails between their legs.

First the little man patted them, stroked them, felt them all over; then, taking out a currycomb, he set about grooming them carefully. And when by dint of combing he had made them as shiny as two mirrors, he put halters on them and led them to market in the hope of selling them and making a nice profit for himself.

And in fact it wasn't long before buyers showed up.

Candlewick was bought by a peasant whose jackass had died the day before; and Pinocchio was sold to the Manager of a circus troupe of clowns and tightrope artists, who bought him in order to train him to jump and dance with the other animals in his company.

And now, my little readers, do you understand what the fine trade carried on by the little man was? From time to time this revolting little monster whose face was all milk and honey would go traveling far and wide with his wagon. Along the way, by means of promises and blandishments he picked up all the lazy boys who didn't like school and books; and after loading them into his wagon, he would drive them to Funland so that they could spend all their time in games, rumpuses, and amusements. When, by virtue of playing all the time and never studying, those poor gullible boys turned into so many donkeys, then all happy and content he would seize them and take them to be sold at fairs and markets. And in this way, within a few years he had made piles of money and had become a millionaire.

What befell Candlewick, I don't know. But I do know that Pinocchio, from the very start, fell into a life of extremely harsh and abusive treatment.

After he was led to the stable, his new master filled his manger with straw; but after tasting a mouthful of it, Pinocchio spat it out.

Then the master, grumbling, filled the manger with hay; but he didn't like the hay either.

"Ah, so you don't care for hay either?" the master shouted, flying into a rage. "Leave it to me, my pretty donkey; if you've got fancies in your head, I know how to get rid of them."

And to teach him a lesson, he cracked the whip against the donkey's legs.

Pinocchio began to cry and bray with pain; and braying, he said:

"Hee-haw! Hee-haw! I can't digest straw!"

"Then eat the hay," retorted his owner, who understood the Asinine dialect quite well.

"Hee-haw! Hee-haw! hay gives me a bellyache."

"Do you expect me to feed a jackass like you breast of chicken and capon in aspic?" added his master, growing angrier all the time and giving him a second lash with the whip.

After this second lash, Pinocchio, out of prudence, immediately became silent and said no more.

Then the stable door was closed, and Pinocchio was left alone. But because he hadn't eaten for many hours, he began to yawn with hunger. And in yawning he opened his mouth so wide that it looked like an oven.

Not finding anything else in the manger, he finally resigned himself to chewing some hay; and after chewing it long and well, he shut his eyes and swallowed it.

"This hay isn't bad," he said then to himself, "but how much better it would have been if I had gone on studying! Instead of hay, now I could be eating a piece of fresh bread and a nice slice of salami. Well, it can't be helped now!"

On waking up the next morning, he immediately looked in the manger for some more hay; but he didn't find any, because he had eaten it all up during the night.

So then he took a mouthful of chopped straw; but while he chewed away at it, he was forced to admit that the taste of chopped straw wasn't at all like that of rice or macaroni.

"Well, it can't be helped now!" he said again, continuing to chew. "But at least let my misfortune serve as a lesson to all disobedient children and to those who don't want to study. So be it! So be it!"

"So be it, my foot!" bellowed the master, coming into the stable at that moment. "Do you by any chance think, my pretty little donkey, that I bought you just to give you food and drink? I bought you so you'd work and help me make a lot of money. So come on, then; there's a good fellow! Come into the ring with me, and I'll teach you how to jump through hoops, burst headfirst through paper barrels, and dance the waltz and polka standing on your hind legs."

Whether he liked it or not, poor Pinocchio had to learn all these fine tricks; but in order to learn them it took him three months of training and a lot of whippings that almost took the hair off his hide.

Finally, the day came when his master was able to announce a truly exceptional event. Posters of various colors, pasted at street corners, read like this:

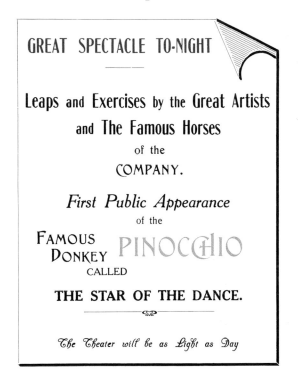

GREAT SPECTACLE TO-NIGHT

Leaps and Exercises by the Great Artists and The Famous Horses of the COMPANY.

First Public Appearance of the

FAMOUS DONKEY PINOCCHIO CALLED

THE STAR OF THE DANCE.

The Theater will be as Light as Day

That evening, as you may well imagine, the house was crammed full an hour before the show was to begin.

There wasn't an orchestra seat left to be had, nor a place in the loges, nor a box; not even by paying its weight in gold.

The gallery tiers were swarming with children, with girls and boys of all ages who were in a fever of excitement waiting to see the famous donkey Pinocchio dance.

When the first part of the show was over, the circus Manager, dressed in a black tailcoat, white tights, and high leather boots extending above the knee, came before the packed audience; and after making a deep bow, he very solemnly declaimed the following ludicrous speech:

"Honorable public, cavalieres and noble ladies! Your humble undersigned passing through this illustrious metropolitan, I determined to procreate myself the honor not to mention the pleasure of presenting to this intelligent and conspicuous audience a celebrated donkey who formerly had the honor of dancing in the presence of His Majesty the Emperor of all the principal Courts of Europe.

"And by way to thank you, assist us with your animating presence and bear with us."

This speech was received with a great deal of laughter and much applause; but the applause redoubled and became a virtual storm at the appearance of the donkey Pinocchio in the middle of the ring. He was all primped up smartly. He had a new bridle of patent leather with brass studs and buckles, two white camellias at his ears, his mane divided into a lot of ringlets tied with pretty red silk tassels, a broad gold-and-silver sash around his middle and his tail braided with purple and sky-blue velvet ribbons. In short, he was a donkey to steal your heart away.

In introducing him to the public, the Manager added these words:

"My worthy auditors! I will not here make mention of the mendacious difficulties suppressated by me in order to reprehend and subjugate this mammal while he was grazing freely from mountain to mountain in the plains of the torrid zone. Observe, I beg you, how much wild game transudes from his eyes, for inasmuch and insofar as all means of taming him to the life of civilized quadrupeds having proved vainglorious, I was obliged several times to resort to the amiable language of the whip. But every kindness of mine, instead of endearing me to him, has only won him over to me. I, however, following the system of Wales, found a

small bony Carthage in his cranium, which the Medicean Faculty of Paris itself declared to be the bulb that regenerates hair and the pyrrhic dance. And for this reason I decided to train him in dancing, let alone the relative jumps through hoops and paper-sheathed barrels. Esteem him! And then judge him! However, before taking my lease from you, allow me, ladies and gentlemen, to invite you to tomorrow night's matinee. But in the apotheosis that the rain should threaten wet weather, then the show, instead of tomorrow night, will be postponed until tomorrow morning, at eleven A.M. in the afternoon."

And here the Manager made another very deep bow; then, turning to Pinocchio, he said:

"Come now, Pinocchio! Before beginning your feats, hail this worthy audience—cavalieres, noble ladies, and children!"

In obedience, Pinocchio quickly bent his two front knees to the ground and remained kneeling until the Manager, cracking his whip, cried out to him:

"Walk!"

Then the donkey got up on his four legs and began to go around the ring, walking steadily at a slow pace.

After a while the Manager cried:

"Trot!" And Pinocchio, in obedience to the command, shifted his pace into a trot.

"Gallop!" And Pinocchio went into a gallop.

"Charge!" And Pinocchio started to charge at full speed. But while he was speeding like a racehorse, the Manager raised his arm in the air and fired off a pistol.

At that shot, the donkey, pretending to be wounded, fell full-length in the ring as though he were really dying.

After he had raised himself from the ground amid an explosion of cheers, shouts, and clapping that rose to the stars, he instinctively lifted his head to look up...and as he looked, he saw in one of the boxes a beautiful lady who had around her neck a thick gold chain from which hung a medallion. On the medallion was the portrait of a puppet.

"That's my portrait! That lady is the Fairy!" said Pinocchio to himself, recognizing her at once; and allowing himself to be overcome with great joy, he tried to cry out:

"Oh, my dear Fairy; oh, my dear Fairy!"

But instead of these words, out of his throat came a bray so loud and so long that it made all the spectators laugh, especially all the children who were in the theater.

Then the Manager, in order to teach him a lesson and make him understand that it's not good manners to go around braying in the public's face, gave him a rap on the nose with the handle of his whip.

The poor little donkey stuck his tongue way out and licked his nose for at least five minutes, thinking perhaps that in this way he could wipe away the pain he felt.

But how great was his despair when, turning his gaze upward a second time, he saw that the box was empty and that the Fairy had vanished!

He felt as though he would die; his eyes filled with tears and he began to weep bitterly. However, nobody noticed it, least of all the Manager who, on the contrary, cracked his whip and cried out:

"There's a good fellow, Pinocchio! Now you'll show these ladies and gentlemen how gracefully you can jump through the hoops."

Pinocchio made two or three attempts, but whenever he came up to the hoop, instead of going through it he found it more convenient to duck under it. Finally, he made a leap and went through it, but unluckily his hind legs got caught in the hoop, so that he fell to the ground in a heap on the other side.

When he got up again, he was lame and could hardly make it back to the stable.

"Bring out Pinocchio! We want the donkey! Bring out the donkey!" shouted the children from the orchestra floor, moved and much distressed by that pitiful accident.

But the donkey wasn't seen anymore that evening.

The following morning, after the veterinarian—that is, the animal doctor—had examined him, he declared that he would be lame for life.

So the Manager said to his stable boy:

"What do you expect me to do with a lame jackass? He'd be a useless sponger eating for nothing. So take him to the square and sell him."

When they reached the square, right away they found a buyer who asked the stable boy:

"How much do you want for that lame donkey of yours?"

"Twenty dollars."

"I'll give you twenty pennies. Don't think I'm buying him to have him work for me; I'm buying him only for his hide. I see he has a tough hide, and I want to make a drum with it, for my village band."

I leave it to you, children, to imagine what a great pleasure it was for poor Pinocchio when he heard that he was destined to become a drum.

So it was that as soon as the buyer had paid the twenty pennies, he led the donkey to the seashore; and after putting a stone around his neck and tying one of his legs with a rope that he held onto with his hand, he suddenly gave him a shove and threw him into the water.

With that stone around his neck, Pinocchio quickly sank to the bottom; and the buyer, holding the rope tightly in his hand, sat down on a rock, giving the donkey all the time he needed to drown to death so that he could then skin him and remove his hide.

Thrown into the sea, Pinocchio is eaten by fish and becomes a puppet as before; but while he is swimming to safety, he is swallowed by the terrible Whale.

After the donkey had been underwater for fifty minutes, the buyer said to himself: "By this time my poor lame donkey must be good and drowned. Let's drag him back up and make that fine drum with his hide."

So he began pulling up the rope that he had tied to the donkey's leg; and he pulled and pulled and pulled until at last he saw appearing on the surface of the water…can you guess what? Instead of a dead donkey, he saw come to the surface a live puppet who was wriggling like an eel.

Seeing that wooden puppet, the poor man thought he was dreaming and stood there dumbfounded, with his mouth wide open and his eyes popping out of his head.

When he had recovered a little from his initial shock, amid his crying and stammering he said:

"But where's the donkey I threw into the sea?"

"I'm that donkey," answered the puppet, laughing.

"You?"

"Me!"

"Ah, you cheat! Are you trying to make a fool of me?"

"Make a fool of you? By no means, dear master; I really mean what I'm saying."

"But how is it possible that you who were a donkey a short while ago have now turned into a wooden puppet just by being in the water?"

"It must be the effect of the seawater. The sea plays tricks like that."

"Watch out, puppet, watch out! Don't think you can amuse yourself at my expense. It'll be too bad for you if I lose my temper!"

"Well then, master; do you want to know the whole story? Untie this leg for me, and I'll tell you."

That fine oaf of a buyer, being curious to know the true story, quickly undid the knot in the rope that kept the puppet bound; and then Pinocchio, finding himself as free as a bird in the air, went on to say as follows:

"Well, the fact is that I was a wooden puppet, just as I am now, but I was on the verge of becoming a boy like any other boy in the world; however, because of my dislike for school and because I listened to bad companions, I ran away from home…and then one fine day, when I woke up, I found myself changed into a jackass with enormous ears…and a long, long tail. What a humiliation that was for me! Such a humiliation, dear master, that I pray blessed Saint Anthony may never let even you experience it. Taken to the donkey fair to be sold, I was bought by the Manager of a company of performing horses who took it into his head to make a great dancer and a great hoop-jumper of me; but one night, during the performance, I had a nasty fall and remained lame in both legs. Then the Manager, not knowing what to do with a lame donkey, sent me to be sold again, and you bought me."

"Unfortunately! And I paid twenty pennies for you. And now who's going to give me back my poor twenty pennies?"

"And why did you buy me? You bought me to make a drum out of my hide! A drum!"

"Unfortunately! And now where can I find another hide?"

"Don't give up all hope, master. There are plenty of donkeys in this world!"

"Tell me, you impudent brat, is that the end of your story?"

"No," replied the puppet, "another word or two, and then it'll be over. After buying me, you led me to this place to kill me; but then, yielding to a humane feeling of compassion, you preferred to tie a stone around my neck and throw me into the sea. Such an exquisite sentiment does you great honor, and I will be forever grateful to you for it. However, my dear master, you reckoned without the Fairy this time."

"And who is this Fairy?"

"She's my mother, and she's like all those good mothers who love their children deeply and never lose sight of them and who help them lovingly in all their troubles, even when these children, because of their recklessness and bad ways, would fully deserve to be abandoned and left to shift for themselves. As I was saying, then, as soon as my good Fairy saw me in danger of drowning, she quickly sent an immense shoal of fish around me; and they, taking me truly for a dead donkey, began to eat me up. And what huge bites they took! I would never have thought that fish were greedier than boys. Some ate my ears, some ate my muzzle, some my neck and mane, some the skin of my legs, some the coat of my back; and among them there was one little fish who was so amiable that he even went so far as to eat my tail."

"From now on," said the horrified buyer, "I swear I'll never taste fish again. I wouldn't be exactly pleased to open a red mullet or a fried hake and find a donkey tail inside."

"I'm of the same opinion," replied the puppet, laughing. "Anyway, the fact is that when the fish had finished eating all that donkey hide that covered me from head to foot, they naturally came to the bone, or rather to the wood; because, as you can see, I'm made of especially hard wood. But after taking just a few bites, those greedy fish soon discovered that wood wasn't meat for their teeth, and disgusted by such indigestible food they went off, some one way, some another way, without even looking back to thank me. And there you have the explanation of how it was that when you pulled in the rope you found a live puppet instead of a dead donkey."

"I don't give a fig for your story," shouted the buyer, flying into a rage. "I know that I spent twenty pennies to buy you, and I want my money back. Do you know what I'll do? I'll take you back to the market and resell you for your weight in seasoned wood, good for kindling a fire in the hearth."

"Go ahead and resell me; it's all right with me," said Pinocchio.

But as he said this, he took a great leap and splashed into the middle of the water; and as he swam merrily farther and farther away from shore, he shouted to the poor buyer:

"Farewell, master! If you ever need a skin to make a drum, think of me."

And he laughed and went on swimming. And after a little while, turning around he shouted still louder:

"Farewell, master! If you ever need some seasoned wood to kindle a fire in the hearth, think of me."

So it was that in the twinkling of an eye he had gone so far that he could hardly be seen anymore; or rather, all that could be seen on the surface of the sea was a small black speck that every once in a while raised its legs out of the water and cut capers like a dolphin in a sportive mood.

While he was swimming along aimlessly, Pinocchio saw a rock that seemed made of white marble there in the middle of the sea, and on top of the rock was a pretty little She-Goat who was bleating tenderly and beckoning him to come near.

The most curious thing of all was that the pretty Goat's hair, instead of being white or black, or spotted with those two colors like that of other goats, was all blue—but such a radiant blue that it very much recalled the hair of the beautiful Little Girl.

I'll leave it to you to guess whether poor Pinocchio's heart began to beat faster. Redoubling his efforts he began swimming toward the white rock; and

he was already halfway there when suddenly there rose from the water the horrible head of a sea monster that came at him with its mouth yawning like a chasm, and there were three rows of long sharp teeth that, even in a picture, would have been terrifying to see.

And do you know who that sea monster was?

The sea monster was neither more nor less than the gigantic Whale referred to several times in this story and who, because of his insatiable appetite and the havoc he wreaked, had come to be nicknamed "the Attila of Fish and Fishermen."

Just imagine poor Pinocchio's terror at the sight of that monster. He tried to avoid him, to change his course, to get away. But that enormous, gaping mouth kept coming at him with the speed of lightning.

"Hurry, Pinocchio, for mercy's sake!" the pretty little Goat bleated loudly.

And Pinocchio swam desperately with his arms, with his chest, with his legs and feet.

"Be quick, Pinocchio, for the monster's getting closer!"

And gathering all his strength, Pinocchio strained twice as hard in the chase.

"Look out, Pinocchio! The monster's catching up with you! There he is! There he is! Hurry, for mercy's sake, or you're lost!"

And Pinocchio swam faster than ever, on and on and on, like a rifle shot. And already he was near the rock, and now the little Goat, hanging as far as she could over the water, was holding out her little hoofs to help him out of the sea.... But!

But by then it was too late! The monster had caught up with him. Drawing his breath in, the monster sucked in the poor puppet as easily as he would have sucked a hen's egg. And he swallowed him with such vehemence and with such greed that Pinocchio, falling into the belly of the Whale, landed with so rude a jolt that he lay dazed for a quarter of an hour.

When he came to after the shock, he couldn't figure out where in the world he was. All around him there was total darkness, so deep and black a darkness that he felt as if he had gone headfirst into a full inkwell. He listened carefully, but he didn't hear a sound. However, from time to time he felt strong gusts of wind smacking against his face. At first he couldn't understand where the wind came from, but then he realized that it came from the monster's lungs. Because, you see, the Whale suffered badly from asthma; and when he breathed, it was just as if the north wind were blowing.

At first Pinocchio did his best to keep his courage up, but when he knew for a fact beyond all doubt that he was trapped in the belly of the sea monster, he began to bawl and scream:

"Help! Help! Oh, poor me! Won't anybody come to my rescue?"

"Whom do you expect to rescue you, unlucky fellow?" said a cracked, harsh voice in the darkness, sounding like an untuned guitar.

"Who's that speaking?" asked Pinocchio, frozen with terror.

"It is I! I am a poor Tuna, swallowed by the Whale along with you. And what kind of fish are you?"

"I don't have anything to do with fish. I'm a puppet."

"Well then, if you're not a fish, why did you let yourself get swallowed by the monster?"

"I didn't let myself be swallowed; he just went and swallowed me! And now what are we going to do here in the dark?"

"Accept the situation, and wait for the Whale to digest us both."

"But I don't want to be digested!" bellowed Pinocchio, beginning to cry again.

"I'd rather not be digested, either," continued the Tuna, "but I'm enough of a philosopher to console myself with the thought that when one is born a Tuna there's more dignity in dying under water than under oil."

"That's ridiculous!" shouted Pinocchio.

"That's my opinion," replied the Tuna, "and opinions, as all Tuna politicians say, are to be respected."

"Well, I want to get out of here; I want to escape."

"Escape, if you can."

"Is this Whale that has swallowed us very big?" asked the puppet.

"Just figure that his body is more than a mile long, without counting his tail."

While they were carrying on this conversation in the dark, Pinocchio saw what he thought was a glimmer of light far, far away.

"What can that little light far, far away there be?" said Pinocchio.

"It's probably one of our companions in distress, waiting his turn like us to be digested."

"I want to go and see him. Who knows? It might be some old fish able to tell me the way to escape."

"I hope so for your sake, with all my heart, dear puppet."

"Good-bye, Tuna."

"Good-bye, puppet, and good luck."

"Where shall we meet again?"

"Who knows? It's better not even to think about it!"

In the Whale's belly Pinocchio finds…whom does he find? Read this chapter and you will know.

ight after he had bidden adieu to his good friend Tuna, Pinocchio set out gropingly in the midst of that darkness, and feeling his way along the inside of the Whale, he advanced one step at a time toward the faint light that he saw glimmering far, far off.

And as he walked, he felt his feet splashing in a pool of greasy, slippery water that gave off such an acrid smell of fried fish.

And the farther he advanced, the brighter and more distinct the glimmer of light became, until after walking and walking, he finally got to it; and when he did get to it…what did he find? I'll give you a thousand guesses: he found a small table laid for a meal, with a burning candle stuck in a green glass bottle on it; and sitting at the table was a little old man, all white as though he were made of snow or whipped cream, who was chewing with difficulty on some small live fishes so very alive that even while he was eating them, they would sometimes leap right out of his mouth.

At that sight poor Pinocchio was seized by such a great and unexpected joy that he practically became delirious. He wanted to laugh, he wanted to cry, he wanted to say so many many things; but instead he mumbled indistinctly and stammered a few broken incoherent words. Finally, he succeeded in letting out a shout of joy; and opening his arms wide, he threw himself around the old man's neck and began to exclaim:

"Oh, dear, dear father! At last I've found you again! Now I'll never leave you again, never, never again!"

"Then my eyes do not deceive me?" replied the old man, rubbing his eyes. "Then you're really my own dear Pinocchio?"

"Yes, yes, it's me, really me! And you've already forgiven me, haven't you? Oh, dear Father, how good you are! And to think that instead I.... Oh, but if you only knew how many misfortunes have fallen on my head and how many things have gone wrong for me! Just think that on the day you sold your jacket, poor dear Father, and bought me the spelling book so that I could go to school, I ran away to see the puppets, and the puppeteer wanted to put me into the fire to roast his mutton, he was the one that gave me five gold coins to bring to you, but I came across the Fox and the Cat who took me to the Red Crawfish Inn where they ate like wolves, and when I left alone at night I met the assassins who started to chase after me, and I ran away with them behind me, and I kept on running and they kept right behind me, and I kept running, until they hanged me from a branch of the Great Oak, which was where the beautiful Little Girl with blue hair sent a carriage to get me, and the doctors, after they had examined me, said right away: 'If he's not dead, it's an indication that he's still alive,' and then a lie slipped from me and my nose began to grow and couldn't pass through the bedroom door anymore, which is why I went with the Fox and the Cat to bury the four gold coins, since I had spent one at the Inn, and the Parrot began to laugh, and instead of two thousand coins I didn't find anything, which when the Judge found out that I had been robbed he had me put in jail right away to compensate the thieves, from where, when I came out, I saw a beautiful bunch of grapes in a field, but I got caught in an animal trap, and the peasant with all the right in the world put a dog collar on me so that I'd guard his chicken coop, but he recognized my innocence and let me go, and the Serpent, with his tail smoking, began to laugh and burst a vein in his chest, and so I went back to the house of the beautiful Little Girl, who was dead, and seeing me cry the Pigeon said to me: 'I saw your father building a little boat to go and look for you,' and I said: 'Oh, if I only had wings too!' and he said: 'Do you want to go to your father?' and I said: 'Oh, do I! But who'll take me there?' and he said: 'I'll take you to him,' and I said: 'How?' and he said: 'Climb on my back,' and so we flew all night, then in the morning all the fishermen who were looking out to sea said to me: 'There's a poor man in a boat who's drowning,' and from far away I recognized you immediately, because my heart told me it was you, and I signaled to you to come back to shore."

"I recognized you, too," said Geppetto, "and I would have been glad to get back to shore, but what could I do? The sea was rough, and a big wave overturned my boat. Then a horrible Whale who was nearby no sooner saw me in the water than he rushed toward me, stuck out his tongue, caught me up neatly, and swallowed me as if I were a tart."

"And how long have you been trapped in here?"asked Pinocchio.

"Ever since that day. It must be two years by now. Two years, my dear Pinocchio, that have seemed like two centuries to me."

"But how have you managed to survive? And where did you find the candle? And who gave you the matches to light it?"

"I'll tell you everything now. The fact is that the same storm that upset my boat also caused a merchant ship to sink. All the sailors were saved, but the ship sank to the bottom; and this same Whale, who had a splendid appetite that day, after swallowing me, also swallowed the ship."

"What? He swallowed it whole in one mouthful?" asked Pinocchio, astounded.

"All in one mouthful; and he spat out only the mainmast, because it had got stuck between his teeth like a fishbone. Quite fortunately for me, the ship was loaded not only with tins of preserved meat, but also with hardtack, that is, ship biscuits, bottles of wine, raisins, cheese, coffee, sugar, tallow candles, and boxes of wax matches. With all that bounty from heaven, I've been able to survive for two years. But now I'm down to the end; now there's nothing left in the pantry, and this candle you see lit is the last one I have left."

"And then?"

"And then, my dear boy, we'll both be left in the dark."

"Then there's no time to lose, dear Father," said Pinocchio. "We have to think about getting away right now."

"Getting away? But how?"

"By escaping through the Whale's mouth, and throwing ourselves into the sea."

"That's easy for you to say, dear Pinocchio, but I don't know how to swim."

"What does that matter? You can get astride my shoulders, and since I'm a strong swimmer, I'll bring you safe and sound to the shore."

"You're dreaming, my boy!" replied Geppetto, shaking his head and smiling sadly. "Do you think it's possible that a puppet, barely three feet tall, as you are, can have enough strength to swim with me on his shoulders?"

"Give it a try, and you'll see! In any case, if it's written in heaven that we must die, at least we'll have the great consolation of dying clasped together."

And without another word Pinocchio took the candle in his hand; and lighting the way as he went ahead, he said to his father:

"Follow me, and don't be afraid."

And thus they walked a long way, traversing the whole belly and the whole length of the Whale's body. But when they reached the point where the monster's spacious throat began, they decided to stop and take a look so as to seize the right moment for their escape.

Now you should know that because the Whale was very old and suffered from asthma and palpitations of the heart, he was obliged to sleep with his mouth open, so that when Pinocchio came to where his throat began and looked up he could see on the outside of that enormous gaping mouth quite a bit of starry sky and very bright moonlight.

"This is the right moment to escape," he whispered then, turning to his father. "The Whale is sleeping like a dormouse, the sea is calm and it's as clear as day. So follow me, dear Father, and in a little while we'll be safe."

Without further ado they climbed up the sea monster's throat, and after arriving at the huge mouth they began to walk on tiptoe along his tongue—a tongue so wide and so long that it resembled a large garden lane. They were just on the point of taking the great leap into the sea to swim away, when, right then, the Whale sneezed, and in sneezing he gave such a violent jolt that Pinocchio and Geppetto were bounced back and catapulted once more into the pit of the monster's body.

In the heavy impact of the fall, the candle went out and father and son were left in the dark.

"And now?" asked Pinocchio, becoming somber.

"Now, my boy, we're really done for."

"Why are we done for? Give me your hand, dear Father, and be careful not to slip."

"Where are you taking me?"

"We must try again to escape. Come with me, and don't be afraid."

With these words Pinocchio took his father by the hand, and walking all the while on tiptoe, together they went up again through the monster's throat; then they traversed the length of his tongue and surmounted his three rows of teeth. Before taking the great leap, however, the puppet said to his father:

"Climb astride my shoulders and hold your arms around me very tight. I'll take care of the rest."

As soon as Geppetto had settled himself firmly on his son's shoulders, good Pinocchio fearlessly threw himself into the water and began swimming. The sea was as smooth as oil, the moon was shining in all its splendor, and the Whale went on sleeping so soundly that not even a cannon shot would have awakened him.

CHAPTER XXXVI

At last Pinocchio ceases to be a puppet and becomes a boy.

hile Pinocchio was swimming hurriedly to reach the shore he noticed that his father, who was astride his shoulders and had his legs half in the water, was shivering hard, as if the poor man were stricken with malaria.

Was he shivering with cold or with fear? Who knows? Perhaps a little of each. But Pinocchio thought that the trembling was from fear, and in order to comfort him he said:

"Take heart, Father! In a few minutes we'll reach land and be safe."

"But where is this blessed shore?" asked the old man, getting more and more worried and squinting just as tailors do when they thread a needle. "I've been looking all around, but all I see is sky and sea."

"But I see the shore, too," said the puppet. "Let me tell you, I'm like a cat; I see better by night than by day."

Poor Pinocchio was pretending to be in high spirits, but instead...instead he was beginning to lose heart. His strength was giving out, his breathing was becoming heavy and labored...in short, he was worn out and the shore was still far off.

He swam until he was out of breath; then he turned to Geppetto and spoke in a broken voice:

"Father...save yourself...for I'm dying!"

And father and son were now just about to drown when they heard a voice like an untuned guitar that said:

"Who is it that's dying?"

"I am, and my poor father."

"I recognize that voice! You're Pinocchio!"

"Quite right, and you?"

"I'm the Tuna, your prison mate in the Whale's belly."

"But how did you manage to escape?"

"I followed your example. You're the one who taught me the way; and after you, I got away too."

"Dear Tuna, you've shown up just in time! I beg you by the love you bear your little tuna children, help us or we're lost."

"Willingly, and with all my heart. Hang onto my tail, both of you, and let me tow you. In four minutes I'll get you to shore."

As you can well imagine, Geppetto and Pinocchio accepted the offer at once, but instead of hanging onto his tail, they thought it would be more convenient if they got right on the Tuna's back.

"Are we too heavy?" Pinocchio asked him.

"Heavy? Not in the least; I feel as if I had a couple of empty seashells on me," answered the Tuna, who was so big and sturdy in build that he looked like a two-year-old bullock.

On arriving at the shore, Pinocchio was first to jump down, in order to help his father do the same. Then he turned to the Tuna and said to him in a voice full of emotion:

"My friend, you've saved my father! I can't find words to thank you enough. Allow me at least to give you a kiss as a sign of my eternal gratitude."

The Tuna stuck his snout out of the water, and Pinocchio, kneeling down to the ground, bestowed a most affectionate kiss on his mouth. At this show of spontaneous and most heartfelt tenderness, the Tuna, who wasn't used to that sort of thing, was so moved that, lest he be seen crying like a baby, he ducked his head under the water again and disappeared.

Meanwhile, day had dawned.

Then Pinocchio, offering his arm to Geppetto, who barely had the strength to stand on his feet, said to him:

"Just lean on my arm, dear Father, and let's go on. We'll go little by little, just as ants do, and when we're tired we'll rest along the way."

"But where are we to go?" asked Geppetto.

"In search of a house or a hut, where out of charity somebody might give us a piece of bread and some straw to lie on."

They hadn't yet gone a hundred steps when they saw two ugly mugs sitting by the side of the road and begging for alms.

It was the Cat and the Fox, but they were no longer recognizable from before. Just imagine, the Cat, by having pretended for so long to be blind, had ended up really going blind; and the Fox, now old, mangy, and completely paralyzed on one side, didn't even have his tail anymore. So it is. The wretched swindler, having fallen into the most abject misery, finally was forced to sell even his magnificent tail to a peddler, who bought it to make himself a fly whisk.

"Oh, Pinocchio," cried the Fox in a whining voice, "give some alms to us two poor invalids."

"Invalids!" repeated the Cat.

"Farewell, pretty masqueraders!" the puppet answered. "You tricked me once, but you won't fool me again."

"Believe me, Pinocchio, now we're poor and miserable for real!"

"For real!" repeated the Cat.

"If you're poor, it serves you right. Remember the proverb that says: 'Stolen money brings no gain.' Farewell, pretty masqueraders!"

"Have pity on us!"

"On us!"

"Farewell, pretty masqueraders! Remember the proverb that says: 'The devil's grain yields naught but chaff.'"

"Don't desert us!"

"...sert us!" repeated the Cat.

"Farewell, pretty masqueraders! Remember the proverb that says: 'He who steals his neighbor's cloak is bound to die without a shirt.'"

And with that, Pinocchio and Geppetto continued calmly on their way until, after having gone another hundred steps, they saw at the end of a country lane in the middle of the fields a charming hut all made of straw, but with its roof covered with tile and bricks.

"That hut must be inhabited by somebody," said Pinocchio. "Let's go there and knock."

In fact, they went and knocked at the door.

"Who is it?" said a little voice from within.

"It's a poor father and a poor son, without bread and without a roof over their heads," answered the puppet.

"Turn the key and the door will open," said the same little voice.

Pinocchio turned the key, and the door opened. As soon as they went in they looked all around, but they didn't see anybody.

"But where's the owner of this hut?" said an amazed Pinocchio.

"Here I am, up here!"

Father and son looked up quickly toward the ceiling, and there, on a joist, they saw the Talking Cricket.

"Oh, my dear little Cricket," said Pinocchio, greeting him politely.

"So I'm your 'dear little Cricket' now, am I? But do you remember when you threw a mallet at me to chase me out of your house?"

"You're right, dear Cricket! Chase me away now...throw a mallet at me now, too; but have pity on my poor father."

"I'll have pity on the father and on the son, too; but I wanted to remind you of the nasty turn I received from you, so as to teach you that in this world we must be kind to everybody, whenever we can, if we want to be repaid with equal kindness in time of need."

"You're right, dear Cricket; you're more than right, and I'll remember the lesson you've given me. But will you tell me how you managed to buy this charming hut?"

"This hut was given to me as a gift yesterday by a pretty Goat whose hair was of a very beautiful blue color."

"And where has the Goat gone?" asked Pinocchio with burning curiosity.

"I don't know."

"But when will she come back?"

"She's never coming back. She went away yesterday, quite sad and bleating as if to say: 'Poor Pinocchio, I'll never see him again; by now the Whale must have eaten him all up.'"

"Did she really say that? Then it was her! It was her! It was my dear little Fairy!" Pinocchio began to exclaim, sobbing and weeping bitterly.

When he had had a good cry, he dried his eyes, and having prepared a nice little bed of straw, he made old Geppetto lie on it. Then he asked the Talking Cricket:

"Tell me, dear Cricket, where can I find a glass of milk for my poor father?"

"Three fields away from here there's Giangio, a market gardener, who keeps cows. Go to him and you'll find all the milk you want."

Pinocchio went on the run to the house of Giangio the market gardener; but the market gardener said to him:

"How much milk do you want?"

"I want a full glass."

"A glass of milk costs one penny. So start by giving me the penny."

"I don't have even half a penny," answered Pinocchio, quite humiliated and dejected.

"That's bad, my dear puppet," replied the gardener. "If you don't have even half a penny, I don't have even a drop of milk."

"Never mind!" said Pinocchio, as he turned to go.

"Wait a moment," said Giangio. "We can make a deal between us. Are you willing to turn a windlass?"

"What's a windlass?"

"It's that wooden device that's used for drawing up water from the cistern to water the vegetables."

"I'll give it a try."

"Then draw up a hundred buckets of water for me, and I'll give you a glass of milk in return."

"All right."

Giangio took the puppet into the vegetable garden and showed him how to turn the windlass. Pinocchio got to work right away; but before he had drawn the hundred buckets of water, he was dripping with sweat from head to foot. Never before had he worked that hard.

"Until now, I've had my donkey do this job of turning the windlass," the market gardener said; "but today that poor creature is near death."

"Will you take me to see him?" said Pinocchio.

"Gladly."

As soon as Pinocchio went into the stable, he saw a fine little donkey stretched out on the straw, worn out from hunger and too much work. After he had looked long and hard at him, he became troubled and said to himself:

"Surely I know this little donkey! He looks familiar to me."

And bending down to him, he asked him in the Asinine dialect:

"Who are you?"

At this question the donkey opened his dying eyes and stammered in the same dialect:

"I'm Ca-andle-wi-ick."

Then he shut his eyes again and died.

"Oh, poor Candlewick!" said Pinocchio softly. And picking up a handful of straw, he wiped away a tear that was rolling down his cheek.

"You feel so sorry for a jackass that didn't cost you anything?" said the market gardener. "Then how should I feel, who paid hard cash for him?"

"Well, you see...he was a friend of mine."

"A friend of yours?"

"A schoolmate of mine."

"What?" howled Giangio, breaking into a loud guffaw. "What?! You had jackasses for classmates? I can just imagine the fine education you must have gotten!"

Mortified by those words, the puppet made no reply; he just took his glass of milk, which was still warm, and went back to the hut.

And from that day on, for more than five months he got up faithfully every morning before dawn so as to turn the windlass and earn the glass of milk that did so much good for the delicate health of his father. But he didn't stop at this, for in his spare time he also learned how to weave all kinds of baskets

from rushes; and with the money he gained he provided very sensibly for all their daily needs. Among other things, he built a fine little cart all by himself so as to take his father out on nice days and let him get a breath of fresh air.

And during the evening hours he practiced his reading and writing. In the nearby town, for a few cents he had bought a big book from which the title page and table of contents were missing; and from this he did his reading. As for writing, he used a twig that he sharpened in the manner of a pen; and because he had neither ink nor inkwell, he would dip it into a small vial filled with blackberry and cherry juice.

So it was that by his readiness to use his wits, to work and to get ahead, he not only succeeded in keeping his ailing father in reasonable comfort but was even able to put aside forty pennies to buy some nice new clothes for himself.

One morning he said to his father:

"I'm going to the market near here to buy myself a jacket, a nice cap, and a pair of shoes. When I come back home," he added, laughing, "I'll be so well dressed that you'll take me for a wealthy gentleman."

And when he was outside he began running in high spirits. But all of a sudden he heard himself called by name, and turning around he saw a pretty Snail coming out of the hedge.

"Don't you recognize me?" said the Snail.

"I do, and I don't."

"Don't you remember the Snail who was maid to the Fairy with the blue hair? Don't you remember the time when I came downstairs to let you in and you got your foot stuck in the front door?"

"I remember it all," cried Pinocchio. "Tell me quickly, pretty little Snail, where did you leave my good Fairy? What is she doing? Has she forgiven me? Does she still remember me? Does she still love me? Is she very far from here? Can I go and see her?"

To all these questions asked in a rush and without pausing for breath, the Snail answered with her customary composure:

"My dear Pinocchio, the poor Fairy lies bedridden in the hospital."

"In the hospital?"

"Alas, yes. Plagued by a thousand misfortunes she has become seriously ill and no longer has the money to buy herself a bit of bread."

"Really? Oh, how terribly sad you've made me! Oh, poor dear Fairy! Poor dear Fairy! Poor dear Fairy! If I had a million, I'd run and bring it to her.... But I only have forty pennies.... Here! I was just on my way to buy myself some new clothes. Take these, Snail, and bring them quickly to my good Fairy."

"And your new clothes?"

"What do I care about new clothes? I'd even sell these rags I've got on to help her. Go, Snail, and hurry! But come back here in two days, because I hope to be able to give you some more money. Until now I've been working to support my father; but from now on I'll work five hours more every day so as to support my good mother, too. Good-bye, Snail; I'll expect you in two days."

Contrary to her usual custom, the Snail darted off like a lizard in the torrid days of August.

When Pinocchio returned home his father asked him:

"And your new clothes?"

"I couldn't find any that fitted me well. But that's all right! I'll buy some another time."

That night, instead of staying up until ten o'clock, Pinocchio stayed up working until after midnight; and instead of making eight baskets, he made sixteen.

Then he went to bed and fell asleep. And while he slept, he dreamed that he saw the Fairy, all smiling and beautiful, who gave him a kiss and said:

"Well done, Pinocchio! Because of your good heart I forgive you all the mischief you've done up to now. Boys who take loving care of their parents when they are sick and in need always deserve a great deal of praise and love, even if they cannot be commended as models of obedience and good behavior. Be sensible and good in the future, and you'll be happy."

Here the dream ended, and Pinocchio awoke with his eyes wide open.

Now just imagine his amazement when, upon awaking, he found that he was no longer a wooden puppet, but that he had turned into a boy like all other boys. He gave a look around him, and instead of the usual straw walls of the cottage, he saw a beautiful, cozy room, furnished and decorated with tasteful simplicity. Jumping out of bed, he found a fine new suit of clothes prepared for him, a new cap, and a pair of leather ankle boots that fitted him to perfection.

As soon as he had dressed, he quite naturally put his hands in his pockets, and drew out a little ivory money-case on which these words were written: "The Fairy with blue hair returns the forty pennies to her dear Pinocchio and thanks him so much for his good heart." When he opened the money-case, instead of the forty copper pennies there were forty gold pieces glittering in it, all mint new.

Then he went to look at himself in the mirror, and he thought he was somebody else. He no longer saw the usual image of the wooden marionette reflected there; instead he saw the lively, intelligent image of a handsome boy with chestnut brown hair and light blue eyes, and with a festive air about him that made him seem as happy as a holiday.

In the midst of all these wonders that were following one upon the other, not even Pinocchio himself knew whether he was really awake or whether he was still dreaming with his eyes open.

"But where's my father?" he cried out suddenly; and going into the next room he found old Geppetto—sound, sprightly, and cheerful as in former days—who had already taken up his trade of wood-carver again and was, in fact, designing a beautiful picture frame richly decorated with leaves, flowers, and little heads of various animals.

"Dear Father, satisfy my curiosity for me: what's the cause of all this sudden change?" Pinocchio asked him, throwing his arms around his neck and covering him with kisses.

"This sudden change in our house is all your doing," said Geppetto.

"Why my doing?"

"Because when children go from bad to good, they have the power of making things take on a bright new look inside within their families too."

"And the old Pinocchio of wood, where could he have gone to hide?"

"There he is over there," answered Geppetto; and he pointed to a large puppet propped against a chair, its head turned to one side, its arms dangling, and its legs crossed and folded in the middle so that it was a wonder that it stood up at all.

Pinocchio turned and looked at it; and after he had looked at it for a while, he said to himself with a great deal of satisfaction:

"How funny I was when I was a puppet! And how glad I am now that I've become a proper boy!"

Yours Sincerely
Pinocchio

~Acknowledgments~

e wish to thank the following properties whose cooperation has made this unique collection possible. All care has been taken to trace ownership of these selections and to make a full acknowledgment. If any errors or omissions have occurred, they will be corrected in subsequent editions, provided notification is sent to the compiler.

Vittorio Accornero [Mondadori: Verona, 1942]. Pages 60, 72, 134.

Alice Carsey [Whitman Publishing Co.: Racine Wisconsin, 1916]. Pages 69, 161.

Luigi E. Maria Augusta Cavalieri [Salani: Firenze, 1924]. Pages 21, 64, 87, 100, 114, 132, 153, 164, 170.

Carlo Chiostri [Bemporad: Firenze, 1901]. Pages 22 (bottom), 28, 38, 51, 61, 94, 108, 112, 116, 123, 127, 135, 140, 144, 162.

Charles Copeland [Ginn & Company: Boston, 1904]. Front flap of jacket, pages 22 (top), 63, 65, 91, 111, 152, 158, 160.

Ry Cramer [Publisher unknown: n.d.]. Page 66.

D.M.D. [T.Y. Crowell: New York, 1908]. Page 57.

Ugo Fleres ["Giornale Per I Bambini": Roma, 1881/1883] Page 27.

Charles Folkard [E.P. Dutton & Company: New York, n.d.]. Back cover, back flap of jacket, copyright page, and pages 12, 14, 55, 73, 85, 95, 105, 117, 119, 122, 149, 168, 171.

Gianbattista Galizzi [S.E.I.: Torino, 1942]. Preface and pages 18, 26, 35, 46, 74, 97, 98, 109, 167.

Violet Moore Higgins [Albert Whitman & Company: Chicago, 1926]. Pages 33, 37, 137.

Benito Jacovitti [La Scuola: Brescie, 1943]. Pages 29, 44, 83.

J.K. [Sully & Klenteich: New York, n.d.]. Pages 4, 17.

Maria L. Kirk [J.B. Lippincott Company: Philadelphia, 1916]. Pages 25, 40, 79, 93, 121, 129, 139.

Giuseppe Magni [Bemporad: Firenze, 1890]. Page 45.

Gieorgio Mannini [Bemporad: Firenze, 1931]. Page 84.

Enrico Mazzanti [Felice Paggi: Firenze,1883]. Frontispiece and pages 16, 24, 30, 39, 42, 58, 78, 82, 86, 90, 102, 107, 110, 120, 124, 130, 133, 141, 159.

Attilio Mussino [Bemporad: Firenze, 1911]. Title page and pages 23, 67, 71, 88, 143, 163, 173.

H.G. Nicholas [McLoughlin Brothers: Springfield, Mass., 1938]. Table of contents.

Vesvolod Nicouline [Italgeo: Milano, 1944]. Pages 56, 62, 77, 104.

Maud & Miska Petersham [Garden City Publishing Co.: Garden City, New York, 1932]. Page 154.

Edna Potter [Harper & Brothers: New York, 1925]. Pages 96, 128, 146.

Frederick Richardson [John C. Winston Company: Philadelphia, 1923]. Page 34.

Christopher Rule [J.H. Sears: New York, 1926]. Endpapers.

Tony Sarg [Platt & Monk Co.: New York, 1940]. Front cover and pages 41, 131.

Corrado Sarri [Salani: Firenze, 1929]. Pages 13, 19, 31, 32, 50, 53, 68, 80, 147, 156.

Roberto Sgrilli [Bietti: Milano, 1942]. Pages 49, 150.

Primo Sinopico [Cenobio: Milano, 1946]. Page 157.

Sergio Tofano [Libreria Editrice: Milano, 1921]. Pages 20, 54, 92.

Unknown Artist [Whitman Publishing Co.: Racine, Wisconsin, 1916]. Page 36.